1982
ALFRED A. KNOPF
New York

TON DE JOODE

ANTHONIE STOLK

Illustrated by

KEES DE KIEFTE

THE
BACKYARD
BESTIARY

THIS IS A BORZOI BOOK
PUBLISHED BY ALFRED A. KNOPF, INC.

Text copyright © 1980 by Verbeek & Verbeek Boekpro-
dukties B. V., Eindhoven
Illustrations copyright © 1980, 1982 by Kees de Kiefte/
United Dutch Dramatists
English translation copyright © 1982 by Alfred A. Knopf,
Inc.

English translation by Marian Powell, adapted for the
American edition by Jonathan and Marianna Kastner.

Library of Congress Cataloging in Publication Data

Joode, Ton de.
    The backyard bestiary.

    Revised translation of: Dieren in en om het huis.
    Includes index.
    1. Urban fauna—United States.   I. Kiefte, Kees
de.   II. Stolk, Anthonie.   III. Title.
QL155.J7313   1982   591.909'732   82-47803
ISBN 0-394-52824-7   AACR2

Manufactured in the Netherlands

FIRST AMERICAN EDITION

Contents

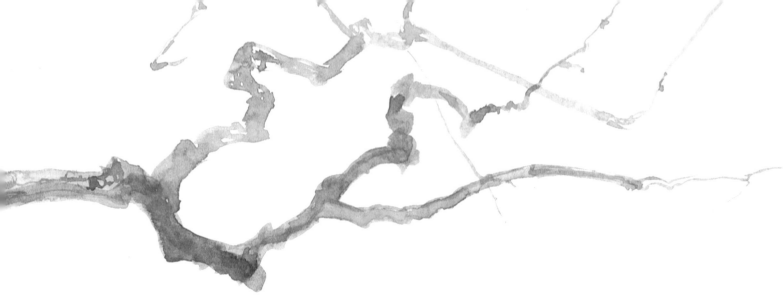

Foreword

In many ways it is animals rather than other humans who are our nearest neighbors. Dogs and cats may actually share our living space, depending on us for food and shelter, rewarding us with companionship; birds hop about on our lawns, sing in our trees, furnish bright spots of color to cheer us in the bleakness of winter. And there are those whose intimacy—while scarcely welcome—may well be even greater: the flea, the housefly, the mosquito, the cockroach. They, as much as human beings, are inhabitants of the "civilized" world. Yet in many cases we know very little about them.

The Backyard Bestiary is a celebration of those creatures, familiar and less well known, that live with us and around us— what they look like, how they behave, odd aspects of their existence (odd only to us, of course), the simple beauty of their bodies, from the frail limbs of the daddy-longlegs to the tough carapace of the tortoise. A cat's eyes glow luminous green in the dark. A toad humps along carrying her mate on her back. A spider methodically contrives a web. Swallows nest in a chimney, a wood louse rolls himself into a tiny armored ball, a ladybug flies away home, a mole tunnels through the soil like some small dry-land submarine. Mammals, birds, amphibians, insects—not one of them is outside our experience, yet at the same time all are rich and strange, full of interest, alive with surprise.

It is in this spirit that *The Backyard Bestiary* has been produced—to provide us not only with facts we need to understand our near neighbors better but also with a keen impression of the delight this knowledge can give us, and a sense of the wonders we live among.

1

A sleepy-looking toad eyes a fly. In an instant it will flick out its tongue and make a meal of the insect.

The Toad

The common toad is a friend to gardeners because it devours insect pests, but to most people it is an ugly and unwelcome sight. Somehow its protruding eyes and bumpy skin, its bloated body and sluggish gait, suggest an evil heart. Over the centuries toads have been linked to witchcraft and to the devil. Witches were once thought to assume the shape of toads, the better to creep into houses via the cellar or well. Farmers thought that toads could suck milk from their cows and goats, and many people believed that they could spray a deadly poison. Some people still believe that they can get warts by touching a toad's skin.

In the matter of poison, toads are not entirely innocent. They do secrete an irritating substance from their salivary glands that, while not deadly, can cause the eyes of a potential predator to burn and tear. A dog that bites a toad and contacts its saliva will feel sick and will salivate profusely. Such an experience may well teach a dog to leave toads alone in the future.

Toads are twilight creatures, coming out mostly at dusk, when it is hard for humans and other predators to distinguish them from the earth they resemble so closely in color and texture. During the day and while hibernating in the winter a toad usually conceals itself. Some use the deserted burrows of small animals, while others dig holes under stones or tree roots with their hind legs.

Despite their bug-eyed appearance, toads

3

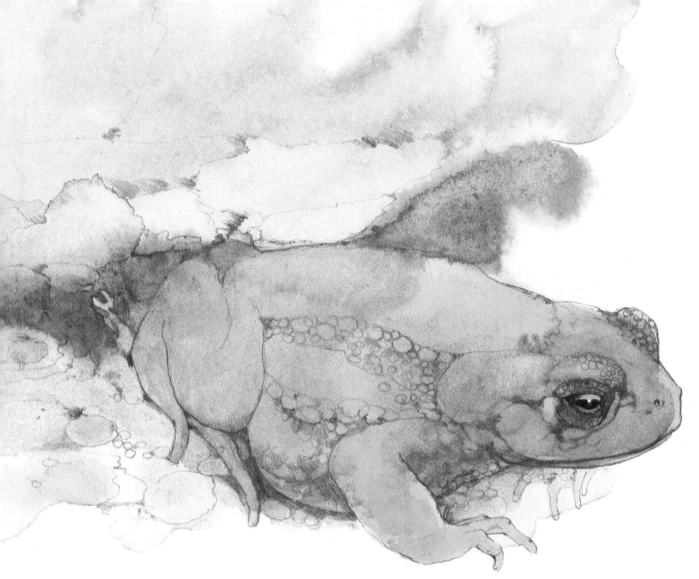

Backed into a burrow under a rock (above), a toad warms up. When the temperature drops below about 45°F, toads must seek warmth. Like all amphibians they are cold-blooded, and regulate their temperature by moving to warmer or cooler places. Toads are fastidious feeders who will scrape the dirt off an earthworm before swallowing it. At right below, a toad splits its outgrown skin with its foot. Next it will shrug its way out, leaving the skin as an eerie symmetrical shadow.

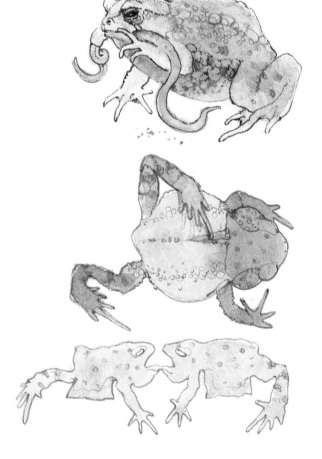

do not see well. Their eyes react only to moving objects, such as the insects that make up much of their diet. Sometimes a toad will catch a twig moving in a breeze, thinking that it has found an earthworm to eat, or while seeking a mate will embrace a clod of mud or a stone instead of another toad. Toads make up for their dim eyesight, however, with lightning-fast tongues that lie coiled like springs in their mouths, ready to be shot out at unsuspecting prey.

One of the strongest driving forces in the

4

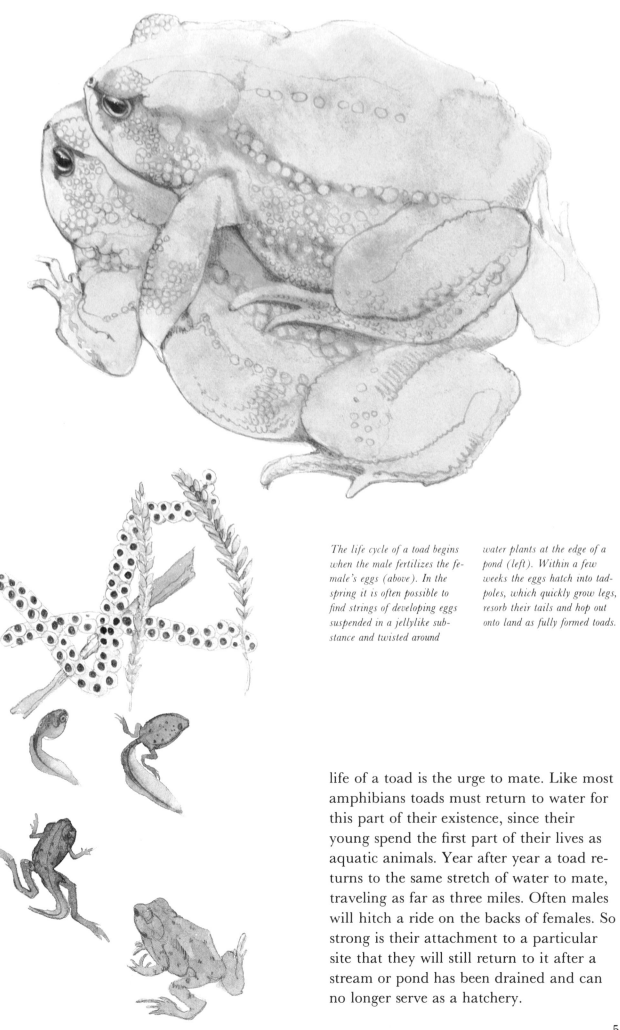

The life cycle of a toad begins when the male fertilizes the female's eggs (above). In the spring it is often possible to find strings of developing eggs suspended in a jellylike substance and twisted around water plants at the edge of a pond (left). Within a few weeks the eggs hatch into tadpoles, which quickly grow legs, resorb their tails and hop out onto land as fully formed toads.

life of a toad is the urge to mate. Like most amphibians toads must return to water for this part of their existence, since their young spend the first part of their lives as aquatic animals. Year after year a toad returns to the same stretch of water to mate, traveling as far as three miles. Often males will hitch a ride on the backs of females. So strong is their attachment to a particular site that they will still return to it after a stream or pond has been drained and can no longer serve as a hatchery.

5

The Robin

In a contest for the title of Most Prevalent North American Bird, the robin would be a strong contender; the familiar red-winged blackbird would be its only serious challenger. Whichever species is the more numerous, there is no doubt about which is the favorite of most people.

Most northern country and suburban residents are cheered out of their winter gloom by the sight of the spring's first robin, one of the first migratory birds to return from the south. Like waxwings and goldfinches, robins migrate during daylight hours, flying farther and farther north as the weather warms (they quite accurately follow average daily temperatures of 37° F). Each year, while lawns and fields are still patchy with snow and last year's grass is brown and shaggy with no hint of new green, the robins strut around looking for spring worms. The males come first, arriving in the northern states in March, but remaining quiet until April. Then, when the females arrive, the males begin to sing—not for joy at the sight of their prospective mates, but in warning to other males to keep out of their territory. The male's song does also serve to attract females; after all, a singing male is one with a territory to protect—a substantial citizen, as it were.

Females usually lay 4 tiny, beautiful turquoise eggs. (It is often possible to find a

A robin (right) clings to a cherry branch before flying off to feed her hungry nestlings a worm (left).

6

A robin cocks its head as if listening for the sound of a worm. Many people believe that they locate worms by hearing them, but experiments have shown that they find them by sight.

lost egg or broken shell under a branch where a robin is nesting.) The female incubates the eggs for 12 to 14 days before the babies hatch out. In another two weeks the young are themselves flying, and the parents are free to raise another brood or two before the season ends and they head south once again for the winter.

The Honey Bee

Among our most useful insect neighbors is one that many people wish we could do without. No one likes to be stung by a bee, but it is a small price to pay for the great work of crop fertilization that honey bees do. These insects center their whole lives on the collection of nectar and pollen from the plants in their habitat. While they are gathering the raw materials to feed their young, they carry pollen from one flower to another, fertilizing all kinds of crops, from

A bee's development (shown in the sequence below) begins when the queen lays an egg in one of the hive's wax cells (left). In 3 days the egg hatches into a larva (second from left), which grows rapidly for 6 days and then spins a cocoon. After 12 days of pupation it emerges from its cell as a fully developed member of the working community.

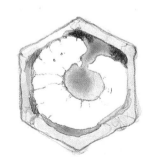
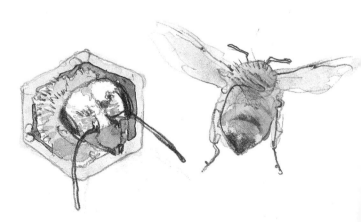

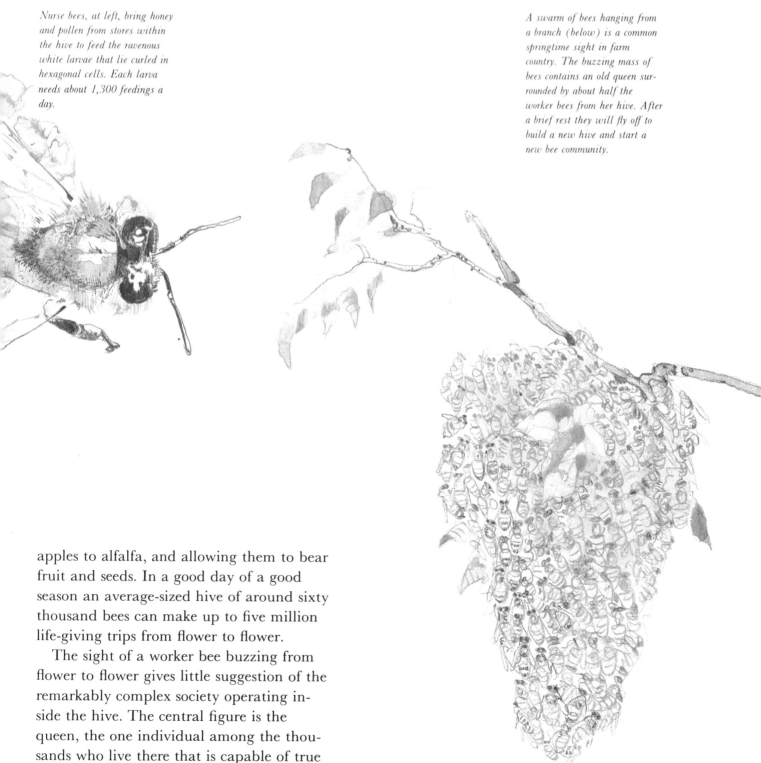

apples to alfalfa, and allowing them to bear fruit and seeds. In a good day of a good season an average-sized hive of around sixty thousand bees can make up to five million life-giving trips from flower to flower.

The sight of a worker bee buzzing from flower to flower gives little suggestion of the remarkably complex society operating inside the hive. The central figure is the queen, the one individual among the thousands who live there that is capable of true reproduction. She spends her life laying eggs—up to 3,000 a day. All the other females in the hive are workers. These bees are basically infertile, but they do occasionally lay eggs. Despite the fact that the eggs are not fertilized, they hatch into drone bees, the males of the hive. Eventually, one drone will fertilize the queen's eggs.

Workers perform a sequence of different jobs during their short lives. For about ten days after they hatch they act as nurses, feeding the developing larvae that will become their coworkers and successors. For another couple of weeks they produce wax from glands under their abdomens, which they use to build and repair the structure of the hive. In their old age—at 3 or 4 weeks— they begin to leave the hive to forage for nectar and pollen, which they process into

A bee gathers nectar and pollen while visiting a lavender thistle flower. Specialized segments of the hind legs, called pollen baskets, enable each worker to carry large loads back to the hive.

honey and pollen cakes, food for the hive's inhabitants. Before long they wear out or meet with an accident and die.

Keeping a group of many thousands of individuals functioning harmoniously for the good of the community requires an excellent system of communication. In the early years of the twentieth century, Austrian biologist Karl von Frisch set out to discover how bees tell each other where to find a good source of food. By marking individual bees with paint and following their travels he discovered that worker bees "dance," to tell other bees when they dis-

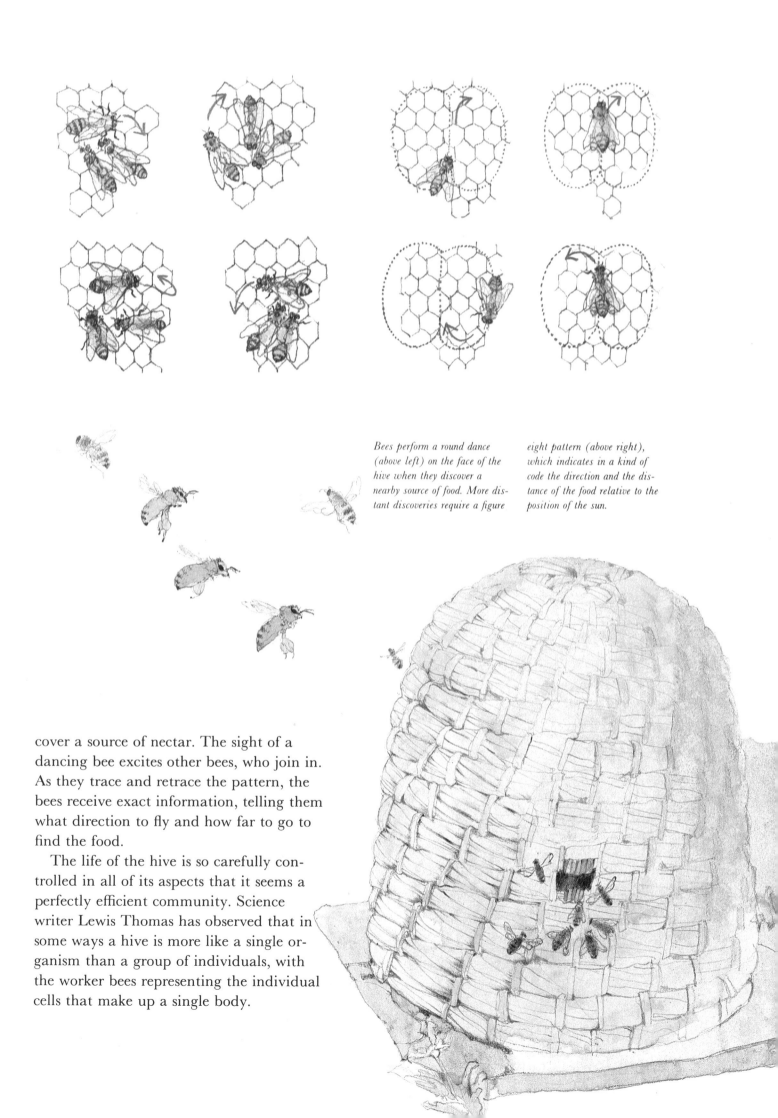

Bees perform a round dance (above left) on the face of the hive when they discover a nearby source of food. More distant discoveries require a figure eight pattern (above right), which indicates in a kind of code the direction and the distance of the food relative to the position of the sun.

cover a source of nectar. The sight of a dancing bee excites other bees, who join in. As they trace and retrace the pattern, the bees receive exact information, telling them what direction to fly and how far to go to find the food.

The life of the hive is so carefully controlled in all of its aspects that it seems a perfectly efficient community. Science writer Lewis Thomas has observed that in some ways a hive is more like a single organism than a group of individuals, with the worker bees representing the individual cells that make up a single body.

The Squirrel

A grey squirrel hanging upside down, skillfully robbing a backyard bird feeder, is the essence of adaptation. Originally, grey squirrels lived in trees, coming down only to gather food and to bury nuts and acorns. Grey squirrels in the wild still live this way, eating seeds from pine cones, mushrooms, even small birds and their eggs, as well as nuts and insects. However, many suburban and city squirrels have found a much easier lifestyle. They grow fat on handouts from humans, eagerly taking bread and seed put out for the birds. Their engaging looks and cheerful manner make it hard for most people to deny them some share of the bounty.

Unlike many of the animals that live in close association with people, grey squirrels do us almost no harm. In fact they help to plant new trees by storing up nuts and seeds, many of which are forgotten or lost before being eaten.

Red squirrels tend to be slightly less tame than the greys, although they are just as delightful to watch as they speed through the trees, jumping from branch to branch. Both types of squirrel make several nests. One is built loosely in the branches of a tree, and is used in warm summer weather. Another is built in a hole in a tree trunk, and serves to keep the animals warm in winter. A

A grey squirrel rests on a branch with its furry tail folded over its back. Roman ladies in ancient times used to keep squirrels for pets, for the pleasure of stroking their soft tails.

third is tightly constructed in the thickest part of a tree's foliage to keep out bad weather. Red squirrels sometimes also build burrows in the ground.

The diets of the two squirrels are similar, but the red's contains more of the seeds found in pine cones. For this reason houses surrounded by evergreens often have a large population of red squirrels, which can make a noisy nuisance of themselves by finding their way into attics and setting up house-keeping. Red squirrels forced to spend the winter outdoors often store up huge caches of pine cones, burrowing through feet of snow to reach them when they need food.

Squirrels have to learn how to crack nuts efficiently. They are born with the innate desire to handle and chew nuts, but only with experience do they discover the weak points of different kinds, and figure out how to open them with the least effort.

13

Tiger swallowtail butterflies are one of the many black and yellow or orange species. Evidently these colors remind predators of stinging insects like wasps and bees, and thus offer the butterflies some protection.

The Butterfly and the Moth

A butterfly's head has a long, coiled proboscis, which is used to extract nectar from deep inside flowers.

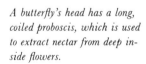
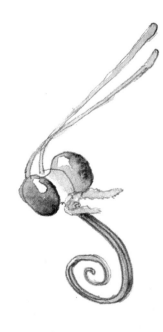

Body color plays a great role in the life of many species of animals, but in none is it more highly developed than in butterflies and moths. Butterflies are active during the day, and their bright colors make them easily seen by such predators as birds. However, in many cases this visibility actually helps the insect survive. Monarch butterflies, for instance, feed on milkweed, which is a poisonous plant, and makes the butter-

14

fly poisonous, too. When a bird eats a monarch, it gets sick. Experiments have shown that once a bird has eaten one it will not touch a monarch butterfly again; it remembers its experience. Since it can easily recognize monarchs by their color pattern, it has no trouble avoiding them.

The viceroy butterfly is marked very much like the monarch, and it benefits greatly from the similarity. Though it is not poisonous, birds mistake it for a monarch and leave it alone, despite the fact that its diet makes it a perfectly tasty morsel for a bird. This method of protection by color imitation requires the sacrifice of a few viceroy individuals every year to young and inexperienced birds that have not yet learned about monarchs. But for the viceroy species as a whole, the deception works very well.

Moths, unlike butterflies, are mostly nocturnal, and therefore most of them are not so brightly colored, having no reason to advertise their presence. Many moths, in fact, take the opposite approach, mimicking with the color and texture of their bodies the surfaces they frequent. Some moths look so exactly like the leaves they feed on that birds hunting for an insect never see them at all. One study done on the color of moths in an industrial area showed that moth coloration

A moth's feathery antennae are richly endowed with odor-receiving cells that can detect a scent from more than a mile away.

A luna moth (left) displays wing spots, which resemble eyes. At right, a swarm of monarch butterflies rest on a branch during their annual southern migration. An individual butterfly may fly up to two thousand miles, from Canada to Mexico and back to the southern United States in one year.

A monarch butterfly's life cycle proceeds from egg, to caterpillar, to chrysalis and finally to mature insect.

can evolve quite quickly over a period of just a few years. During years of increasing pollution the moths became darker and darker to match the background of dirty trees. Presumably the lighter individuals were easy for predators to spot, so that only the darker ones were left to perpetuate themselves. As the area was cleaned up, and air pollution reduced, the moth population reverted to its original lighter color.

Some moths make use of warning colors, as butterflies do. Luna moths, for example, have large spots on their wings, which look like eyes. Normally the moths rest with their wings closed, so that the spots do not show. But when threatened by a predatory bird, they suddenly open their wings, flashing out the "eyes." The bird usually jumps back in fright, associating such large eyes with its own predators—owls and cats.

The Duck

Ducks, both wild and domesticated, are some of mankind's oldest companions. Archeologists have discovered duck bones and human bones together in finds from the time of both ancient Egypt and the Stone Age. People have hunted ducks for food and for sport down through the centuries, and in this country ducks are still shot by the millions as they fly south each fall.

Continental North America is home to about sixty species of duck, the most common of which is the mallard, shown here. Most wild mallards summer in Canada. There the female lays about 8 eggs in a nest she has constructed and lined with down from her body. Usually the nest is located strategically close to water. When her eggs are all laid, she sits on them for about a

A colorful mallard drake preens his feathers while his well-camouflaged mate incubates a nest of eggs.

18

month until they hatch. Baby ducks learn to recognize the sound of their mother quacking and follow her everywhere. She leads them quickly to the nearest water, where they are safer than they are on land. They learn to swim at once.

After mating, and rearing her brood, the female moults, or loses her feathers temporarily. The male may lose his somewhat earlier. For a few weeks after moulting, ducks are unable to fly and have to escape their enemies by swimming away from them.

One of the first species man domesticated was the duck. As many a farmer has discovered, it is easy to tame a duckling if you are there at the moment it hatches. Ducklings, like goslings, attach their affections to the first object they see, and regard it thereafter

Three wild ducks (top) head south on their annual migration from their summer home in Canada to their winter quarters in the southern states, where there is open water. The ducks make good time on their trip: *they have been clocked at up to forty miles per hour. Ducks waterproof themselves by rubbing their bills over a fat-producing gland under their tails, and then wiping the grease across their feathers.*

A mallard hen keeps close watch over her newly hatched brood of ducklings. At first both sexes are marked alike; the males take on their fancy colors when they begin to grow their adult feathers.

as their mother. If they see a person before they see a duck, they will follow him faithfully wherever he goes.

Over the years breeders have developed ducks for different purposes. The white Pekin shown on these two pages was descended, like all species of domestic ducks except the Muscovy, from the wild mallard. Pekins are the breed used to produce the succulent and fast-growing Long Island duckling. Other breeds of domestic duck have been developed to excel as egg layers, or to grow brilliantly colored feathers.

Some of the wild duck's behavior patterns have been lost in the process of domestication. Pekins, for example, cannot fly well enough to migrate in the fall, although many tame ducks become restless in the fall when the wild ducks are migrating, and will keep walking away from home. In many ways, though, domestic ducks still behave like wild ducks: they industriously build

Newly hatched Pekin ducks follow their mother to the water's edge. Conversational even as babies, ducklings peep to each other and to their mother almost constantly.

20

nests, incubate their eggs, and carefully guard and instruct their ducklings, leading them immediately to water, where their ancient instincts tell them that they will be safe. Perhaps it is this enduring combination of wild behavior and total acceptance of man and his ways that has assured the duck its age-old position in the barnyard.

Pekins dive for their dinner, pushing underwater plants around in search of seeds. A duck uses its thick tongue to press food against its serrated upper bill, which acts as a sieve, letting water out and keeping food in.

The Garter Snake

There is probably no animal more harmless than the garter snake. Yet many people hate snakes so much that they kill one whenever they can. Religion may be responsible for some of this prejudice. As if the story of Adam and Eve and the Serpent were not enough by itself, according to the Bible God cursed the entire snake family "above all cattle and above every beast of the field; upon thy belly shalt thou go and dust shalt thou eat all the days of thy life."

Garter snakes, which are the most commonly encountered snakes in North America, live blameless lives as far as humans are concerned. They have no venom; they eat frogs, toads, salamanders and mice, as well as earthworms. Because of their preferred food they tend to live in damp places like marshes and drainage ditches.

In the northern part of the country garter snakes hibernate during the winter, often in large groups. In the southern regions, where the weather is warm enough so that food stays available through the winter, they stay active all year.

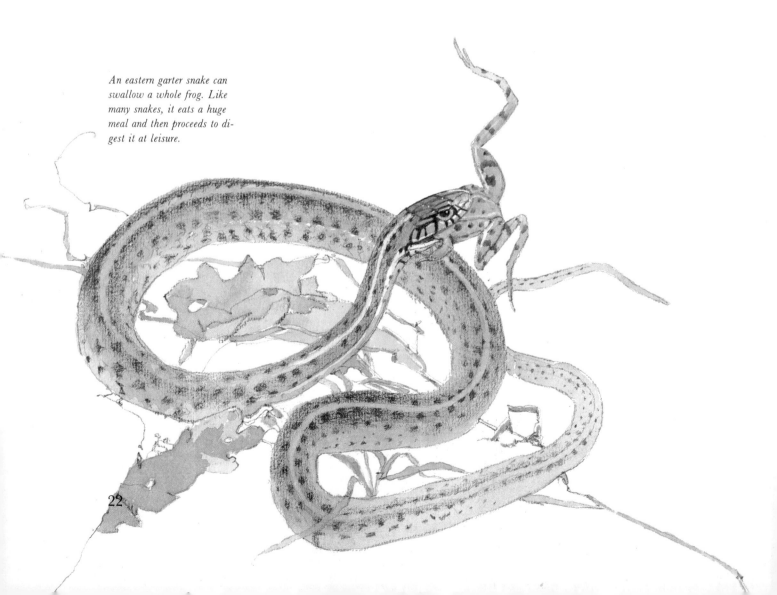

An eastern garter snake can swallow a whole frog. Like many snakes, it eats a huge meal and then proceeds to digest it at leisure.

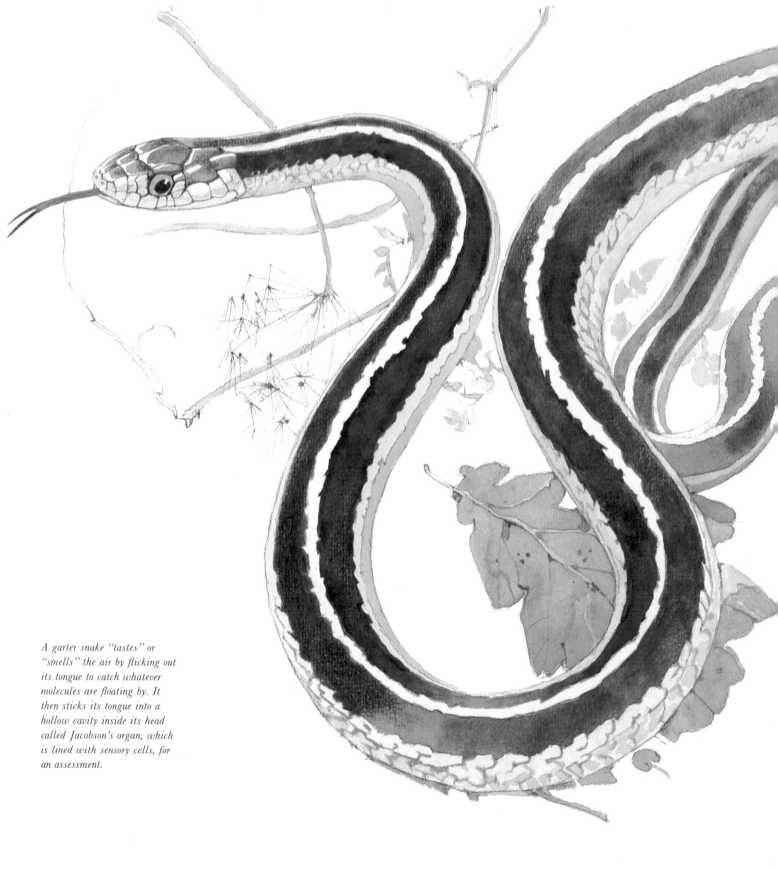

A garter snake "tastes" or "smells" the air by flicking out its tongue to catch whatever molecules are floating by. It then sticks its tongue into a hollow cavity inside its head called Jacobson's organ, which is lined with sensory cells, for an assessment.

There is only one species of common garter snake, but it includes many subspecies, which have quite different markings and color patterns. Identification of an individual snake is made more difficult by the fact that even members of the same subspecies often are marked and colored quite differently. The eastern subspecies, for instance, usually has yellow stripes, but sometimes blue, brown or green ones, and sometimes no stripes at all.

Garter snakes are one of the species of snake that bear their young alive, rather than by laying eggs. The 5- to 9-inch-long young are born between June and August, and take 2 years to reach maturity. The oldest known garter snake lived for 10 years.

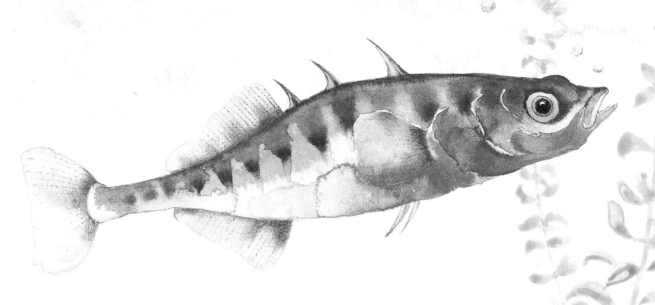

The Stickleback

A common little fish in both salt and fresh waters throughout the Northern Hemisphere, the three-spined stickleback has long fascinated both scientists and aquarium keepers because of the complexity of its reproductive behavior. The species has been so extensively studied both in captivity and in the wild that most of the details of this process are now known.

During the winter, males and females live together peacefully in schools in deep water. As spring approaches, the sexes separate, and the males become aggressive, selecting private territories in shallow water, which they defend. From an inconspicuous stripy green, the colors of the males begin to change: their bellies turn red, a signal to other males to stay away. The males instinctively react to red objects by attacking. The closer they are to the center of their territory the more fiercely they are willing to fight; the male loses his courage as he gets out toward the boundary line.

With his territory firmly established, the male begins to build a nest, scooping out a

At the beginning of the breeding season, two male sticklebacks meet at the frontier of the territories they have claimed. These two fish are shown about three times their actual size.

The curious stickleback reproduction sequence is shown here. First, the male stickleback builds a nest, glueing it together with sticky threads spewed out of his mouth (top). Then he makes a hollow in it (top right) and attracts an

hollow on the bottom of the pond or shore-line and filling it with strands of weed and algae. He glues these together with a sticky thread excreted by his kidneys, and may weigh it down with bits of gravel. He then tunnels through the nest, making it ready to receive the female and her eggs.

The male now becomes even more vividly

egg-filled female with a mating "dance" (left), leading her (right) to his nest. Beginning at left below, he shows her the entrance, she lays her eggs, he fertilizes them and, finally (far right), tends the babies.

colored, a shiny blue top added to his bright red belly. These so-called nuptial colors serve to attract a female. When he sees a female bulging with eggs the male is stimulated to dance a zigzag mating dance in front of her. If she is ready, she turns her head up to indicate acceptance, whereupon he leads her to the nest that he has prepared, twisting over on his side at the entrance to indicate the way in. She swims in and he prods her back with his nose. This causes her to spawn, or shed her eggs, inside the nest.

At this point the female's part in the re-productive process is over, and the male chases her away, taking her place inside the nest to fertilize the eggs. The male may re-peat this process with several females. Then he concentrates his attention on the eggs, which take 1 or 2 weeks to hatch, fanning the nest to bring in a constant supply of fresh water. Once the babies are hatched, he continues his solicitous care, sucking any strays into his mouth and gently returning them to the safety of the nest until they are big enough to fend for themselves.

A domesticated golden hamster, above, cleans his fur while keeping a weather eye on the goings-on of the world outside his cage. Hamsters have large pouches in their cheeks, which they use to carry grains and seeds. At left below, a hamster stuffs seeds into his pouches with his paws. When the pouches are full (middle) they can hold nearly two ounces of food. When he reaches his food storage area (right), he pushes the seeds out, again using his front feet. These small rodents have been known to store up to twenty-five pounds of food in their underground burrows.

The Golden Hamster

The golden hamster is one of the world's most numerous mammals. With a population high in the millions it is popular both as a pet and as a laboratory animal all over the world.

Until relatively recently, however, Western naturalists had never even seen a living specimen. The only indication that such a species had ever existed was the presence of one skin, dating from 1893, in a Beirut, Lebanon, museum. In 1930 Professor I. Abromi of the Hebrew University of Jerusalem dug up a burrow containing one adult female and her twelve young eight feet below the Syrian desert. These animals were first bred in captivity four months later. Scientists believe that the huge captive population that exists worldwide today is descended from this original family.

One of the reasons for the explosive growth of the domestic hamster population can be found in the species' reproductive cycle. Hamsters have the shortest gestation period of any known mammal. It takes only 16 days, on the average, from conception to birth. The female weans her 6 to 12 babies when they are 3 or 4 weeks old, and they

mature in less than 3 months. Since one female can raise 70 to 80 babies a year, it is easy to see how the species grew with such incredible speed in the controlled conditions of the laboratory and breeding farm, where there are no predators.

Little is known about the behavior of hamsters in their natural habitat. Obviously they do not multiply nearly so rapidly as in captivity. Captive specimens have short lives, averaging about 2 years. Presumably, wild hamsters die even sooner under natural conditions. Groups of hamsters live in loosely associated colonies underground, but the members have little to do with each other except when they mate and raise their young. Hamster fanciers can rest assured that this solitary habit of life means that their pets probably do not suffer when they are kept alone in a cage.

Wild hamsters have complex burrows underground, where they dig separate chambers for their nests, their food storage and their droppings. Such fastidious housekeeping makes the little rodents particularly suitable for keeping as pets.

The Spider

Spiders are among mankind's most intimate
associates, but many people are confused
about what part of the animal kingdom
they belong to. They are not insects; rather
they belong to the class Arachnida. They
are closer relatives of scorpions, mites and
ticks than they are of flies and bees. Spiders
have 8 legs instead of 6, and their bodies
are divided into 2 main parts rather than 3.

Among arachnids, spiders are an especially successful and populous group, partly
because of their ability to make silk. All spiders spin cocoons to protect their developing young, and different kinds of spiders use
silk for other purposes as well. The common
garden spider, or orb weaver, uses its silk to
make a web with strong radiating threads
and sticky cross threads for trapping insects.
When a fly or other insect gets stuck, the
spider injects it with poison and wraps it in
silk. Spiders cannot eat solid food; instead
they inject their digestive juices into their
prey, predigesting the contents, and then
suck out the resulting liquid.

Spiders make liquid silk in glands located
in their abdomens. Ducts carry the liquid to
small projections on the back of their abdomens, called spinnerets. Once extruded
from the spinnerets the silk hardens into an
elastic material that, for its weight, is
stronger than steel.

Spiders make a variety of different webs.

The symmetrical web of a com-
mon garden spider is one of na-
ture's great works of art. To its
creator, however, it is a practi-
cal home and trap for its prey.

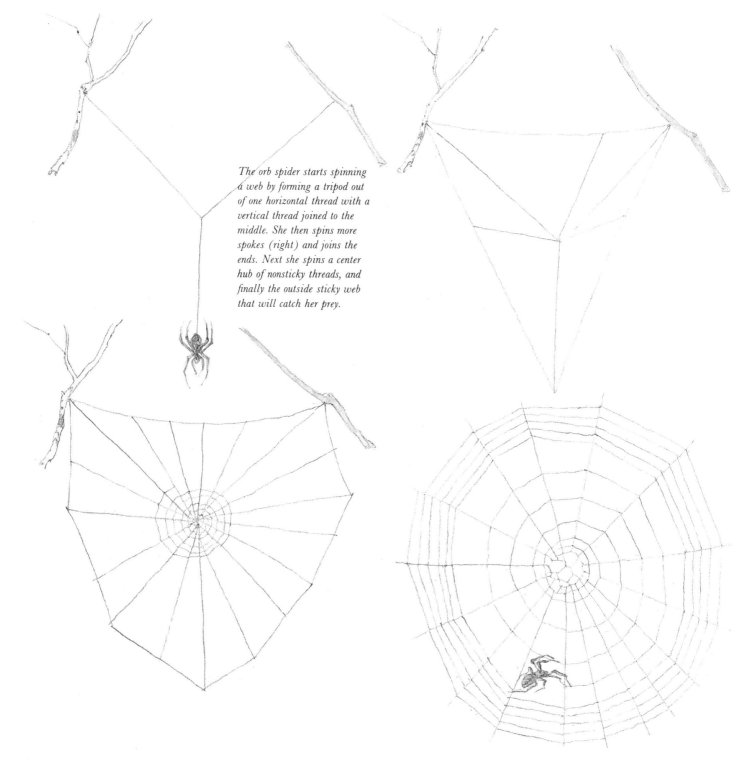

The orb spider starts spinning a web by forming a tripod out of one horizontal thread with a vertical thread joined to the middle. She then spins more spokes (right) and joins the ends. Next she spins a center hub of nonsticky threads, and finally the outside sticky web that will catch her prey.

One family of spiders makes a web specifically designed to trap ants. These spiders hang a series of vertical threads with sticky bottoms attached to the ground. When an ant gets caught on one of the strands, its struggles cause the bottom to snap, and the elastic top jerks the trapped ant into the air. Another kind of spider spins a small web, which it throws over its prey like a net.

Once built, a web serves as more than just an insect trap. It can also be used for communication. A male spider wishing to mate would be unwise just to show up on the female's web, since she regards any movement on the web as a potential meal. He approaches very slowly and carefully, plucking a strand of the web material repeatedly to announce his presence. The garden spider male further ensures his safety by spinning a special mating thread, which he hooks to the center of the web. He lures the female out onto this strand to mate. He then leaves quickly lest he be eaten. In most species of spider, however, the male is not automatically eaten, and can mate with more than one female.

After mating, the female spider lays her eggs and wraps them in a cocoon. Some

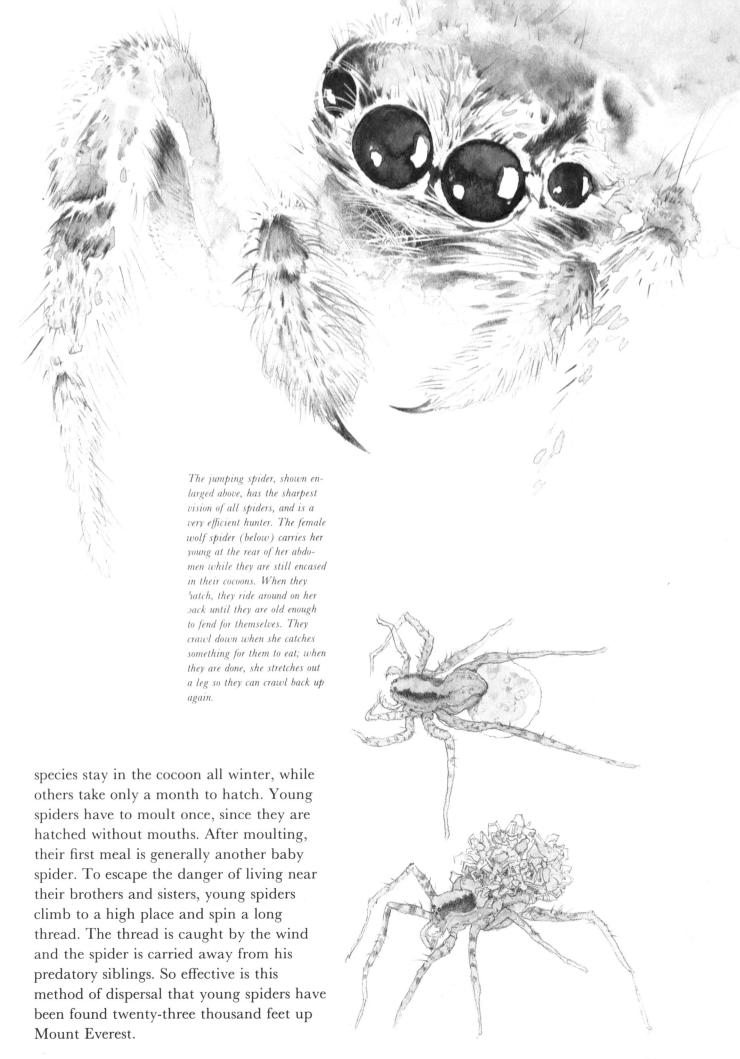

*The jumping spider, shown en-
larged above, has the sharpest
vision of all spiders, and is a
very efficient hunter. The female
wolf spider (below) carries her
young at the rear of her abdomen while they are still encased
in their cocoons. When they
hatch, they ride around on her
back until they are old enough
to fend for themselves. They
crawl down when she catches
something for them to eat; when
they are done, she stretches out
a leg so they can crawl back up
again.*

species stay in the cocoon all winter, while
others take only a month to hatch. Young
spiders have to moult once, since they are
hatched without mouths. After moulting,
their first meal is generally another baby
spider. To escape the danger of living near
their brothers and sisters, young spiders
climb to a high place and spin a long
thread. The thread is caught by the wind
and the spider is carried away from his
predatory siblings. So effective is this
method of dispersal that young spiders have
been found twenty-three thousand feet up
Mount Everest.

The Woodchuck and the Ground Squirrel

Woodchucks are often seen sitting up at the entrance to their burrows, surveying the countryside. Tradition has it that if a woodchuck comes out of its burrow on February 2 and sees its shadow, there will be six more weeks of winter. On the other hand, if the skies are cloudy and it sees no shadow, spring is just around the corner.

In temperate parts of the world, where the summers are warm and the vegetation abundant while the winters are cold and food is scarce, animals have to develop some special technique for surviving through the year. Migratory birds, like robins and finches, solve the problem by wintering where food is more abundant; chipmunks and tree squirrels store food

A thirteen-lined ground squirrel augments its mostly vegetarian diet with a grasshopper.

against leaner times; mice and deer make do by changing their diets to include bark, bulbs and roots instead of the more tasty leaves, buds and grass. Woodchucks and ground squirrels have developed yet another method: they store food in their bodies in the form of fat. All summer long they eat more food than they need, so that by fall they are enormously fat. In September, they descend into their burrows and hibernate. A hibernating woodchuck's metabolic rate slows radically—its temperature falls to about 40°F and its heart beats only 4 times a minute. This saves a great deal of energy. In the northern part of the United States woodchucks hibernate for as much as 8 months of the year.

Woodchucks are hunted heavily in rural areas because their large burrows are damaging to farm machinery. Each woodchuck makes several large holes so that its burrow will have a variety of emergency exits. The larger of these holes can snap the wheel right off a tractor—they are hard to see in tall grass, making them difficult to avoid. And woodchucks are quick to repair any damage to their abodes. One farmer, plowing his field, covered up a woodchuck's hole, and in the short time it took him to finish that furrow and begin the next, the hole had been reopened to its original dimensions. Woodchucks don't endear themselves to gardeners, either, because of their healthy appetite for almost all cultivated plants and their aptitude for digging under fences to get them. Despite their unpopularity, however, woodchucks are quite plentiful—perhaps because they can live to be 15 years old.

In the western states ground squirrels live much the same kind of life as woodchucks. They too become very fat in the fall, but they also store food in their burrows. In the north they go into their burrows at the end of summer, and become dormant, while those in more southern regions stay active most of the year, returning to their burrows only when there is no green feed available.

33

A fight to the death between two male moles may occur during the breeding season when males visit different nests, seeking mates. Often the winner will eat the loser.

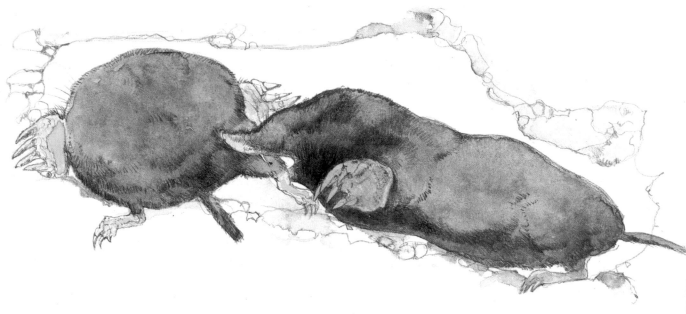

34

A softly furred mole bites into an earthworm, his favorite type of food. Moles also eat insects, larvae, centipedes and other pests. They are voracious feeders, some eating as much or more than their own weight in food each day. In this way they resemble their relatives the shrews.

Bald and white, newborn moles are only the size of kidney beans. Their mothers suckle them for only 4 to 6 weeks, but it takes them up to a year to reach sexual maturity.

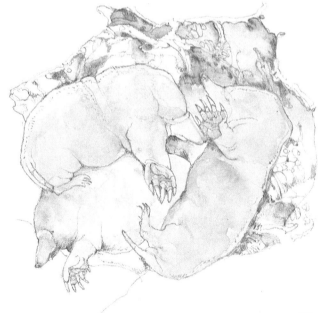

The Mole

Moles are quite common, but they are not among our most frequently encountered animal neighbors because they spend almost all of their time underground. Here they dig elaborately branched and chambered tunnels. Moles make two kinds of tunnel: the shallow runs that are the bane of lawn lovers and golf course greenskeepers, and deeper ones, which are marked on the surface by the small piles of displaced dirt we call molehills. These deep burrows serve as nests and places for raising young, while the shallow ones are places to eat and rest.

Moles have bodies that are so highly spe-

A mole's torpedo shape suits him well for a life spent pushing through tunnels. Even his fur is adapted to his lifestyle, growing in all directions so that he can move forward and backward through his burrows with equal ease.

cialized for their lives underground that they look very different from more familiar, surface-dwelling animals. Having little need to see, moles have nearly dispensed with eyes. Some species have tiny ones, the size of pinheads, that can do little but distinguish between light and dark. In other species skin covers the eyes, blinding the tiny animals completely. They lack external ears, which might collect dirt, but do hear well. To make up for their lack of sight, moles have an extraordinarily well-developed sense of touch. Their blunt muzzles are covered with hundreds of bumps, each containing a bundle of nerve endings. The skin of a mole's abdomen and tail also contains special sense organs. Scientists think that their sense of touch allows moles to detect even the subtle vibrations caused by a crawling earthworm or insect.

No one is quite sure how moles navigate underground. It is known, however, that moles have some way of knowing exactly where they are. If a section of a burrow is crushed, the mole will build a detour joining up exactly with the tunnel on the other side of the earthfall. There must be landmarks underground—perhaps the scent of

certain kinds of soil, vibrations from noises above ground, from other moles digging or from running water. Such landmarks are likely as meaningful to a mole as roads, houses, hills and rivers are to us.

Almost every part of a mole's body has been adapted to a life spent digging. The bones of its front legs and its shoulder girdle are very thick and strong to support the tremendously powerful muscles that move the paws. These muscles are so thick that moles appear to have no neck at all. Their paws are huge in proportion to their overall size. They have 5 strong claws, and the palms are on the back, rather than the front. Thus moles can use their paws like shovels: first

A mole is forced to come above ground to hunt at times when there is a prolonged drought and earthworms are not easy to find. Here he is not so well adapted, and often falls prey to cats, hawks, skunks and the like. Moles have a strong smell, which may repel some predators. Perhaps this is why cats, even when they catch moles, seldom eat them.

they loosen the soil with their claws, then they scoop it around behind and above. Some of the dirt is pressed into the sides of the tunnel, to make it smooth and hard. What is left over ends up as molehills. So efficient are moles at their task that a single animal can plow through several yards of lawn or garden in an hour.

Like rodents, moles will lay up stores of food if they have the opportunity. When there is an extra supply of earthworms, a mole will catch the extras, bite off their heads and store them away. A beheaded earthworm can no longer crawl away, but it remains very much alive, and is thus a source of fresh food. Piles of hundreds of earthworms have been found in storage, their bodies coiled together.

Altogether the rather shy and gentle appearance of moles does not reflect their true character. Like all meat-eaters they are real killers, butchering not only worms and insects, but even good-sized frogs and field mice when the need arises.

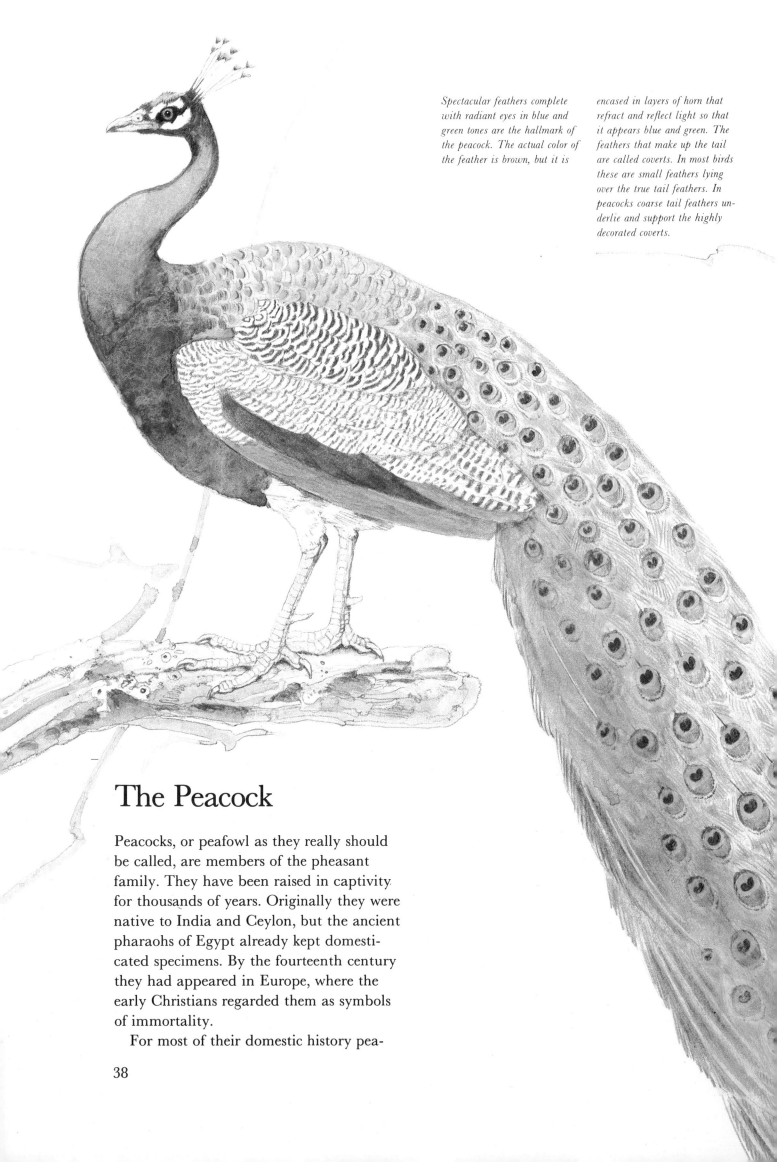

Spectacular feathers complete with radiant eyes in blue and green tones are the hallmark of the peacock. The actual color of the feather is brown, but it is encased in layers of horn that refract and reflect light so that it appears blue and green. The feathers that make up the tail are called coverts. In most birds these are small feathers lying over the true tail feathers. In peacocks coarse tail feathers underlie and support the highly decorated coverts.

The Peacock

Peacocks, or peafowl as they really should be called, are members of the pheasant family. They have been raised in captivity for thousands of years. Originally they were native to India and Ceylon, but the ancient pharaohs of Egypt already kept domesticated specimens. By the fourteenth century they had appeared in Europe, where the early Christians regarded them as symbols of immortality.

For most of their domestic history pea-

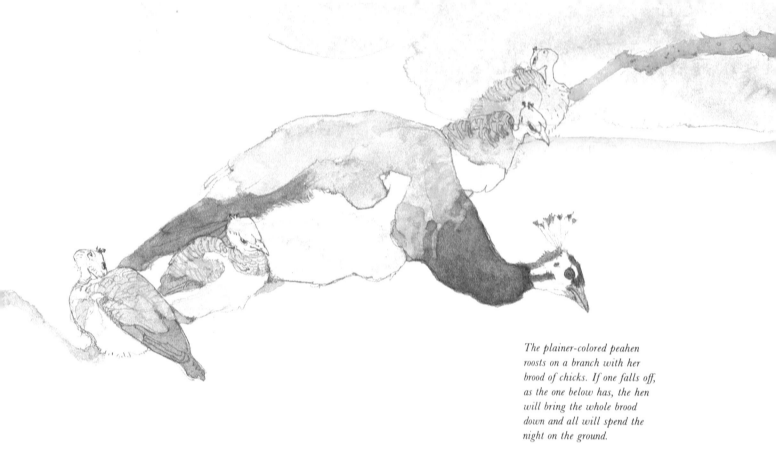

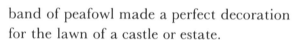

The plainer-colored peahen roosts on a branch with her brood of chicks. If one falls off, as the one below has, the hen will bring the whole brood down and all will spend the night on the ground.

fowl have symbolized pride and perhaps pomposity. This association stems from the behavior of the peacock who, like other flashily colored male birds, displays his feathers and struts around to attract a mate and repel competitors. When a peacock spreads out his enormous fan of feathers it is truly an impressive sight, not only to peahens, but to humans as well. It is easy to see why kings and noblemen thought that a

band of peafowl made a perfect decoration for the lawn of a castle or estate.

In the wild, peafowl live in groups, mainly in forest settings. In the afternoon they begin to move up into the trees, calling to each other with raucous shrieks. Domesticated peafowl behave in much the same way, roosting on roofs and in trees at night, rousing the neighborhood with their incessant squawking.

Peahens lay between 5 and 8 eggs in small depressions, usually under a bush. The mother cares for her brood for about 6 months. When they are a few days old she teaches them to climb to a roosting place at night. It takes a peacock 3 years to reach maturity, at which time he develops his magnificent tail. Even then the feathers have not reached their full brilliance—that takes another 3 years.

Like other members of the pheasant family male peacocks are good fighters. They are equipped with sharp spurs on their legs—when two fight they sometimes both end up dead. Peacocks can turn on other species as well, banding together to attack dogs or other animals that bother them.

The Pigeon

Pigeons are such a common sight in cities and on farms that most people pay no more attention to them than it takes to complain about the mess they make. Some city dwellers like to feed them, while farmers are more likely to contrive ways to keep them out of the hayloft. However, pigeons are ac-tually fascinating birds and are worth studying.

Rock doves, as common pigeons are properly called, are among the fastest flyers in the bird kingdom, reaching speeds of up to eighty or ninety miles per hour. As hom-ing pigeon fanciers know, they also have an

40

incredible ability to find their way home when taken to a distant location. If they are conditioned by being taken farther and farther from home they can return from a distance of one thousand miles.

Much research has been done to find out what navigational aids pigeons use to guide their flight, and apparently there are several. On sunny days they seem to use the sun as a compass, adjusting their course automatically as the sun moves across the sky. There is evidence that on cloudy days they use the earth's magnetic field as a guide.

Pigeons are thought to have been the first domesticated birds. There are terra-cotta figurines from Iraq dating from 4500 B.C. depicting domesticated pigeons, but some historians believe they were bred even earlier, as long ago as the Stone Age. Probably they first were raised for food, and later for their usefulness in carrying messages. Hom-

ing pigeons have played a part in wars for a very long time. Legend has it that pigeon-borne messages informed Rome when Caesar captured Gaul. Alexander the Great sent news of his conquests home by pigeon, while Napoleon used pigeons to bear the bad news from Waterloo. Pigeons served in both world wars—in the Second World War a pigeon named GI Joe won a medal for gallantry because the message he carried saved an Italian village from being bombed.

A young pigeon lives for the first two weeks on "pigeon milk," a substance shed from the mucous membrane lining of the parents' crops. During the last eight to ten days of incubating the eggs, the crops of the parent birds increase twenty times in thickness, under the influence of the hormone prolactin, the same hormone that plays a part in the secretion of milk in cows and other mammals.

Two ants stroke captive aphids, stimulating them to release drops of an excretion called honeydew. Some species of ant tend these leaf-eating insects like cattle, protecting them in exchange for the source of sweet food.

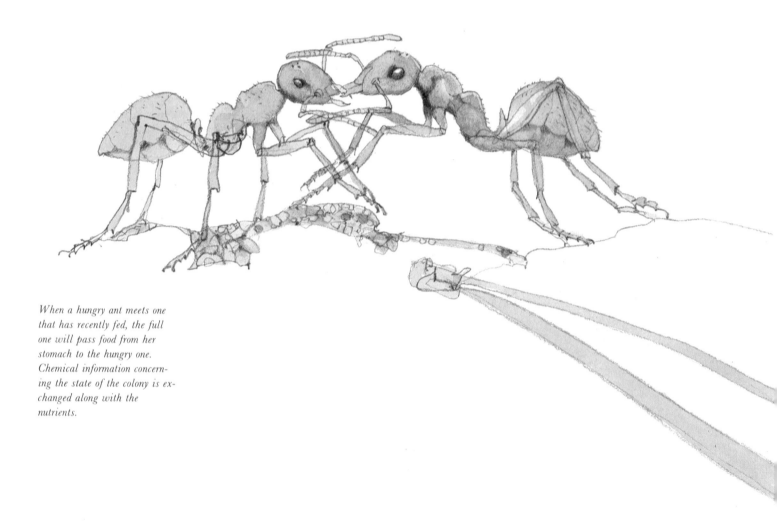

When a hungry ant meets one that has recently fed, the full one will pass food from her stomach to the hungry one. Chemical information concerning the state of the colony is exchanged along with the nutrients.

The Ant

The most common insect on the face of the earth is the ant, and for generations it has been one of the most fascinating to naturalists and other scientists. In the Old Testament King Solomon exhorted, "Go to the ant, thou sluggard; consider her ways, and be wise: which having no guide overseer, or ruler, provideth her meat in the summer, and gathereth her food in the harvest." Like most people, the wise king admired ants for their industry and organized approach to life. In modern times scientists have learned that ants perform most of their feats by in-

stinctive behavior patterns rather than by intelligence, but this fact makes their complex societies no less remarkable.

Ant society is organized in a way similar to that of bee society. At the center of the community is the queen, who may live for 15 years, and who lays all the eggs. Most of her eggs hatch into females—both sterile workers and future fertile queens. Occasionally she lays an infertile egg, which develops into a male. At certain times of year ant colonies produce large numbers of winged males and females. These fly out of the nest

43

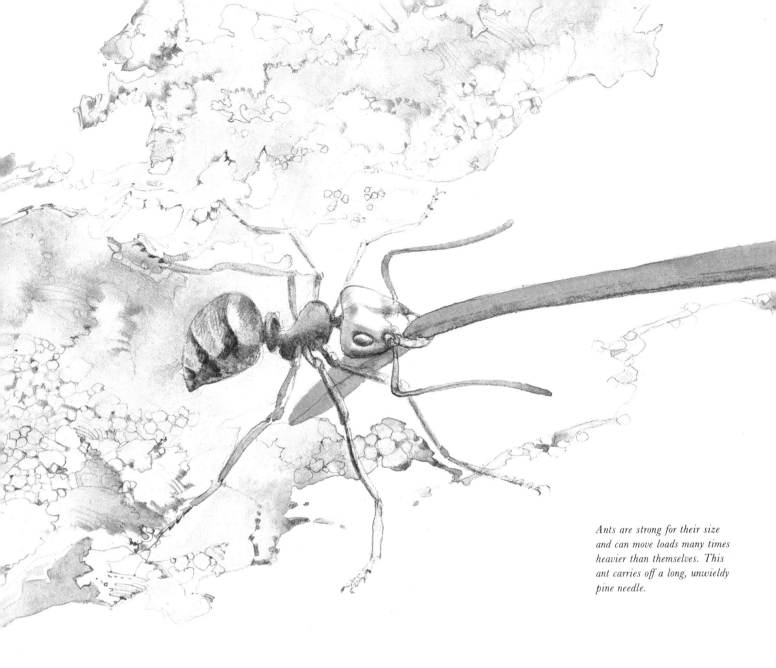

Ants are strong for their size and can move loads many times heavier than themselves. This ant carries off a long, unwieldy pine needle.

and mate. The males die soon afterward; the females become new queens and start new colonies.

Once a queen's first brood of eggs has hatched she no longer has to take care of herself. Her workers feed and groom her, raise her young, maintain and defend the nest, obtain food and tend to all other matters that require action.

In any complex society communication is essential. Ants have developed an interesting way to pass information through the colony. Each ant has a kind of stomach, or crop, which belongs as much to the commu-

nity as it does to herself. When two ants meet they touch mouths and pass to each other a taste of the chemicals that are stored in their crops. These chemicals include food, glandular secretions and chemicals from the stomachs of other ants recently contacted, such as developing larvae or food gatherers from the outside. In this way each ant, whenever it comes into contact with another ant, receives information about the state of the whole colony. Information received in this way directs the behavior of each individual ant.

Different species of ant use this communi-

cation method as the basis for widely differing styles of life. Some ants act like farmers, milking colonies of aphids in exchange for protecting them. Usually this benefits the aphid as well as the ant, but, like human dairymen, ants sometimes use their aphid cattle for meat. Leaf-cutter ants farm in a different way. Members of this species harvest leaves from trees, carry them home and grind them into a moist mass. This substance serves as a growth medium for a kind of fungus that grows in strands. The ants nip off the ends of the strands, which then form a kind of bulb that serves as food for the colony.

There are also species of ant that live much more aggressive lives than the farming species do. Some steal eggs and larvae from other colonies and keep them as slaves when they mature. Army ants make a living as soldiers and killers, rising out of their nests in masses and surrounding prey. In many ways the various ant societies seem like tiny copies of human societies. But there is an important difference: human beings have the intelligence to modify their behavior, while ants are pretty much controlled by inherited responses to the events in their lives.

An ant's heavy jaws allow it to carry large objects, as well as to attack and kill other insects. Some ant bites are powerful enough to be painful to humans.

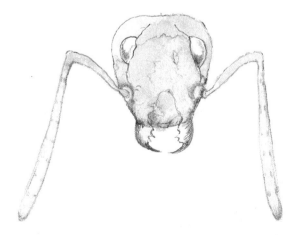

45

The Mouse

Human society, with its warm houses and abundant scraps of leftover food, has created an environment suited for more than just the human species. Mice have been our household companions throughout history, and probably back into prehistory, because they enjoy the same kind of housing, and the same kinds of food, that we do.

Within our walls house mice live in communities where they share eating places, nesting places and dumps for their droppings. They are clean little creatures, grooming themselves frequently, and assisting each other in dealing with hard-to-reach places like the back and the head.

Mice prefer to forage in the dark, and they have developed keen senses that enable them to do so. They mark their trails with urine, leaving a scent that they can follow to find their way back home. When a

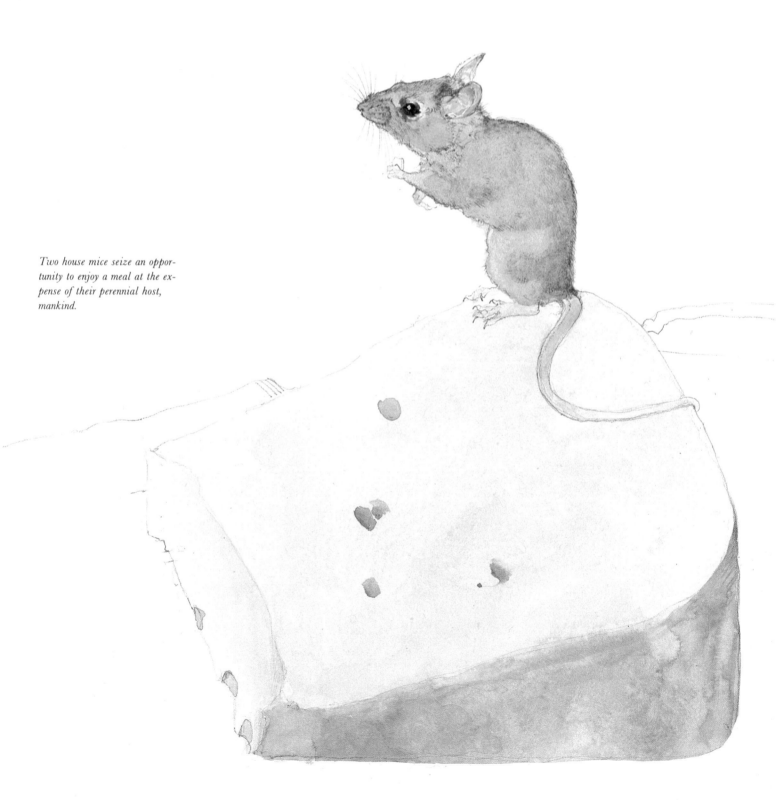

Two house mice seize an opportunity to enjoy a meal at the expense of their perennial host, mankind.

Deer mice form true pairs, one male living with one female. This type of bonding is quite unusual in small mammals.

mouse follows one trail frequently he memorizes every part of it. If he is used to jumping over an obstacle on his route, he will continue to jump over that spot even when the obstacle has been removed. Mice also have a good sense of hearing and can detect sounds of a much higher pitch than the highest sounds we can hear. A young field mouse emits an ultrasonic cry of distress, which will bring his mother instantly to his aid, even if she is busy nursing the rest of her litter. Mice also rely on their whiskers, which are acutely sensitive, to help orient themselves in the dark. When two male mice get into a fight, one may bite off the other's whiskers, leaving him at a great disadvantage.

House mice are not the only ones to live in close association with people. On farms and in the woods there are many other species of mouse. In North and South America there are fifty-five species of white-footed mouse, or deer mouse. They range from Colombia to Alaska, and in their range they are usually the most common mammal present. These prettily marked little mice have adapted themselves to almost every conceivable habitat. The ones that live in the woods tend to be a rich dark brown, while those that live in the open have lighter-colored coats. Mice living near houses often find shelter in their walls during the winter, moving back into the open when spring comes.

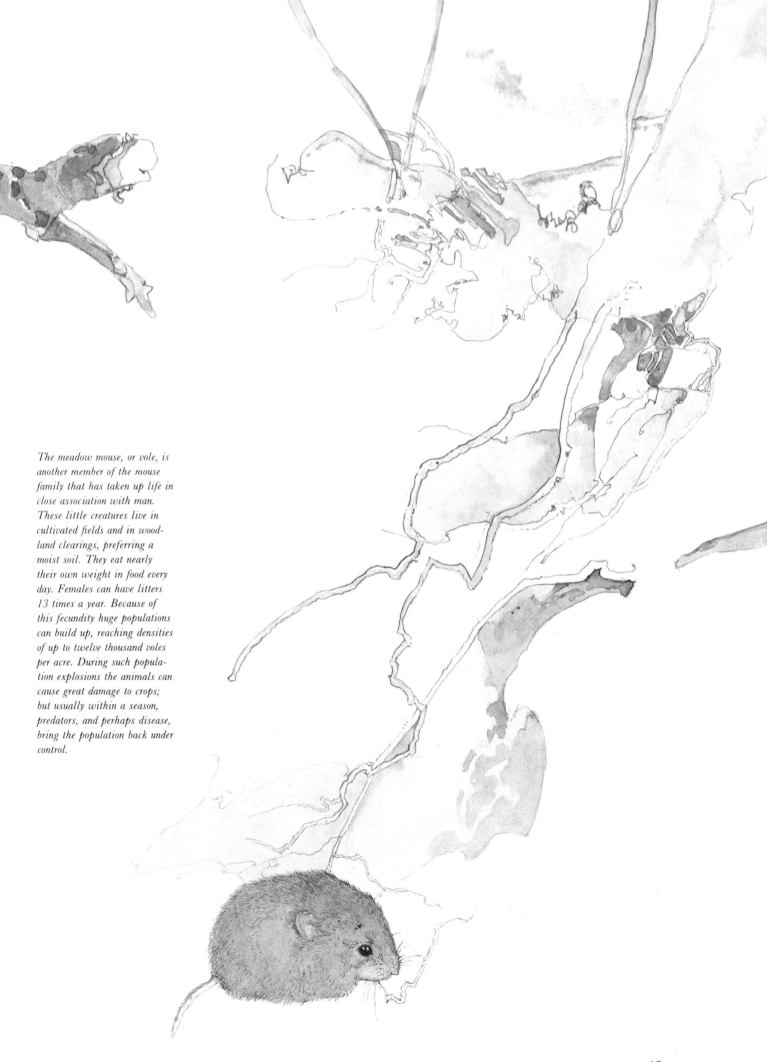

The meadow mouse, or vole, is another member of the mouse family that has taken up life in close association with man. These little creatures live in cultivated fields and in woodland clearings, preferring a moist soil. They eat nearly their own weight in food every day. Females can have litters 13 times a year. Because of this fecundity huge populations can build up, reaching densities of up to twelve thousand voles per acre. During such population explosions the animals can cause great damage to crops; but usually within a season, predators, and perhaps disease, bring the population back under control.

49

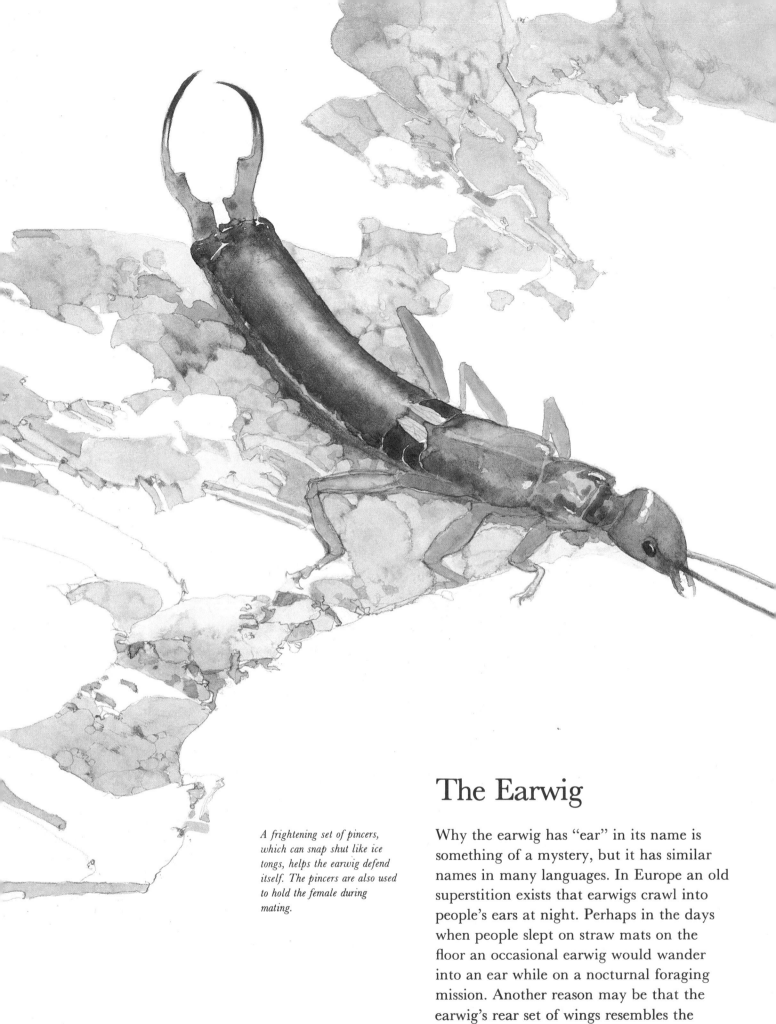

The Earwig

A frightening set of pincers, which can snap shut like ice tongs, helps the earwig defend itself. The pincers are also used to hold the female during mating.

Why the earwig has "ear" in its name is something of a mystery, but it has similar names in many languages. In Europe an old superstition exists that earwigs crawl into people's ears at night. Perhaps in the days when people slept on straw mats on the floor an occasional earwig would wander into an ear while on a nocturnal foraging mission. Another reason may be that the earwig's rear set of wings resembles the shape of human ears.

50

A female earwig makes a pile of her eggs and defends them fiercely.

Female earwigs show a degree of maternal behavior very rare among animals of the simpler orders. They care for their young in a way that we normally associate with higher birds and mammals. A female lays her eggs in the spring. Usually she will place them in a hole in the ground; sometimes she places them under the bark of a tree. While the eggs are developing, she guards them, licking them often to prevent their being eaten by parasites, and chasing off any predators. The eggs take from 2 to 8 weeks to hatch, but even then the mother's job is not over. She continues to guard her young until they have moulted twice and are ready to live on their own. During this time she teaches them how to find food and brings back any youngsters that stray from the group. In some species the mother dies, exhausted, when her young go out on their own, but she provides them with one last service: her body becomes a meal for them.

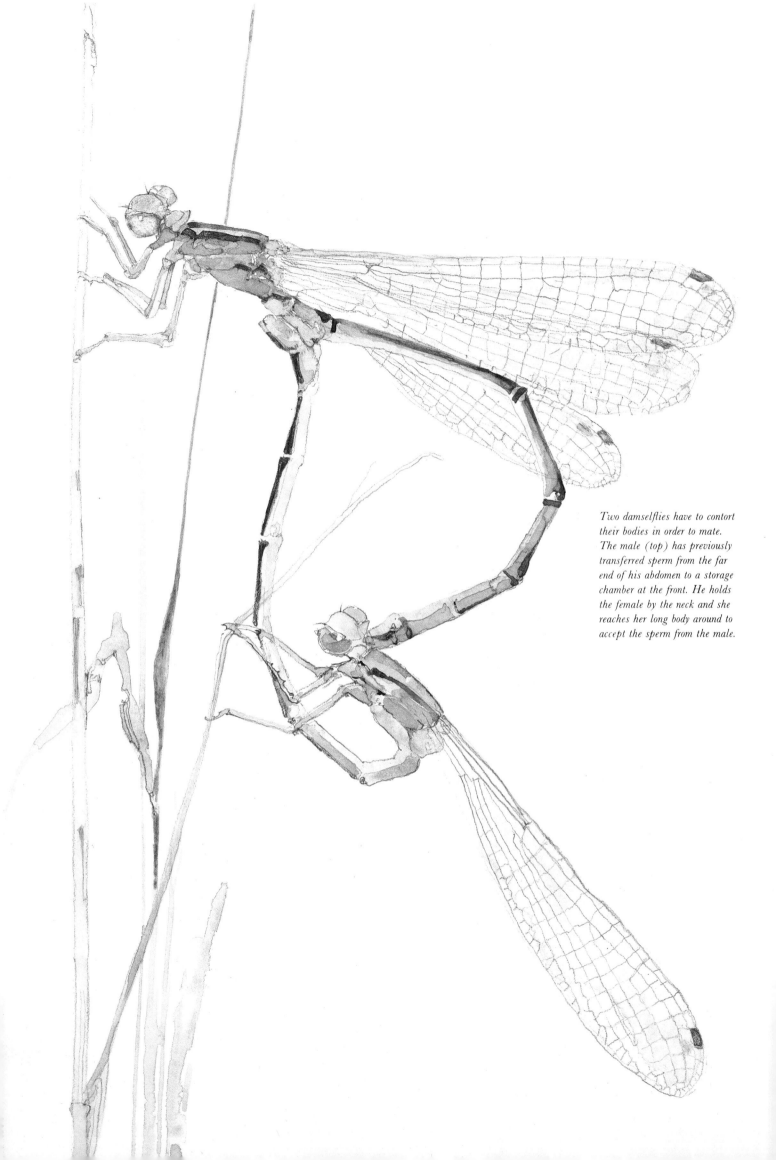

*Two damselflies have to contort
their bodies in order to mate.
The male (top) has previously
transferred sperm from the far
end of his abdomen to a storage
chamber at the front. He holds
the female by the neck and she
reaches her long body around to
accept the sperm from the male.*

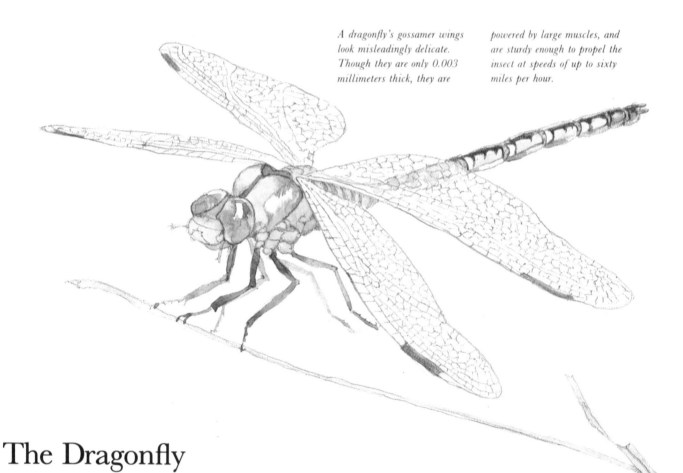

A dragonfly's gossamer wings look misleadingly delicate. Though they are only 0.003 millimeters thick, they are powered by large muscles, and are sturdy enough to propel the insect at speeds of up to sixty miles per hour.

The Dragonfly and the Damselfly

Darting, hovering, and darting off again over the surface of a country pond, a shimmering blue dragonfly hunts smaller insects through a hot summer afternoon. Though it seems too elegantly beautiful to be real, the insect is actually a fiercely efficient predator.

Dragonflies and their close relatives, damselflies, spend the greatest part of their lives underwater. In their immature stages, and even as adults, most species remain close to either a pond or a stream. The female lays her eggs in water, where they fall to the bottom and begin their development. When they hatch, the young spend several years as larvae, eating protozoa and moulting from 10 to 15 times as they grow. They then produce wings and, moulting again, become nymphs, another immature stage. The nymph is a meat-eater, feasting on crustaceans and insect larvae, even on tadpoles and small fish. Finally the nymph stops eating and crawls up on land or onto a water plant and prepares to metamorphose into an adult. It splits out of its exoskeleton, or outer covering, then rests until it is dry. Blood slowly fills the lacy network of veins on its wings, and it is ready to fly off for the final phase of its life cycle.

A dragonfly nymph catches its prey with a huge lower lip called a labium. The lip is hinged and is kept folded up against the bottom of the head when it is not being used. When a suitable meal presents itself, in this case a tadpole, the labium shoots out, grabs the victim, and then serves as a dinner plate, catching any scraps that might fall from the nymph's mouth.

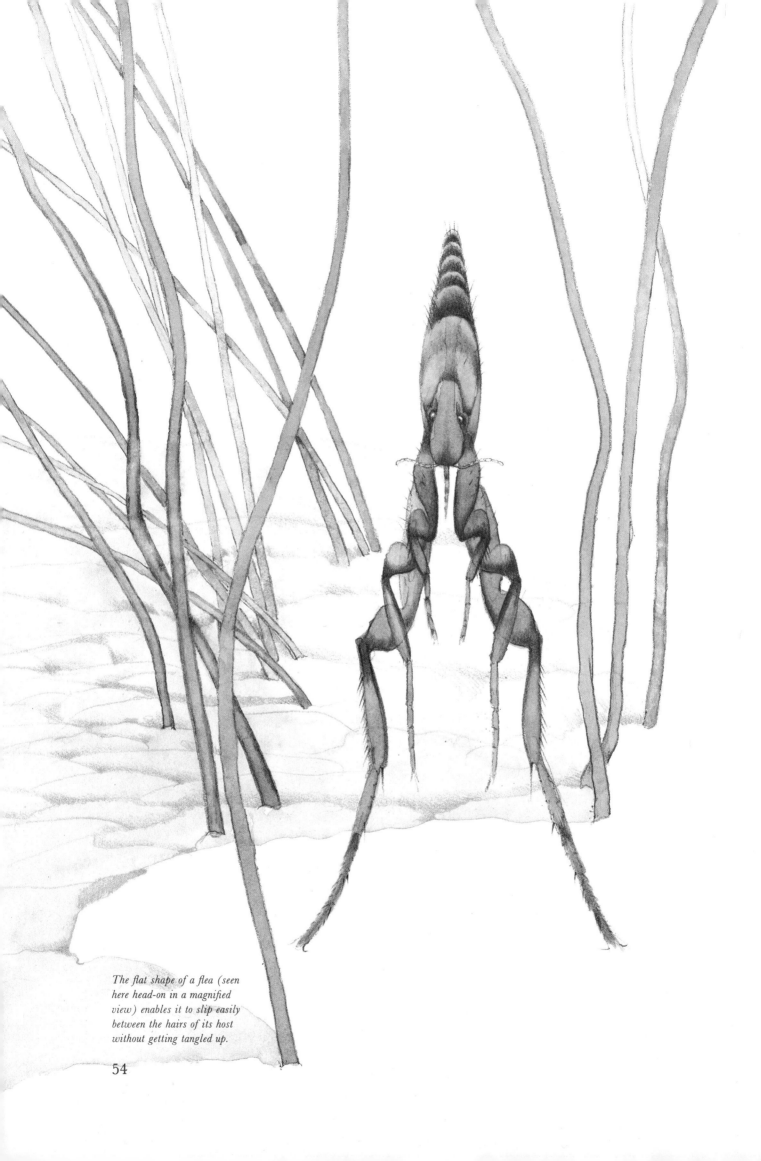

The flat shape of a flea (seen here head-on in a magnified view) enables it to slip easily between the hairs of its host without getting tangled up.

54

The Flea

Some of mankind's closest associates are parasites, and the flea is one whose relationship to us has had tragic consequences. Fleas live by finding a warm-blooded vertebrate such as a human, a bird or a dog, and jumping onto it. Despite the fact that it is only about the size of a pinhead, a flea can jump ten inches, hundreds of times its own height. Once it has found a host, it pierces the skin and fills up on blood, injecting anticoagulants to keep the blood from clotting as the flea drinks.

The bite does little more than annoy the host, and if the flea confined its biting to one individual it would probably not cause much of a problem. But, unfortunately, fleas have large stomachs which can hold a lot of blood and enable them to go without food for some time. Their stomach capacity plus their excellent jumping capability allows them to move easily from one host to another, and even from one species to another. A rat flea, for instance, will make use of a human host if it cannot find a rat. Because of this ability twenty-five million Europeans died in just three years during the fourteenth century. Plague bacillus, which had been endemic in the rat population, became epidemic. Rats that contracted the disease died, and when they did, their fleas moved on to other rats. When rats became scarce, the fleas jumped onto humans instead. The rats could not infect people directly, but the fleas, carrying minute amounts of rat blood in their stomachs, could. When they bit their human host a bit of the plague-infected rat's blood found its way into the host's bloodstream. Sickness and—usually—death followed, and the fleas moved on, spreading bubonic plague wherever they landed.

Improved control of both rats and fleas, as well as the discovery of antibiotics, have prevented major outbreaks of plague in recent times. But small epidemics still occur in tropical countries. Even in this country the plague bacillus continues to live on in some populations of wild rodents.

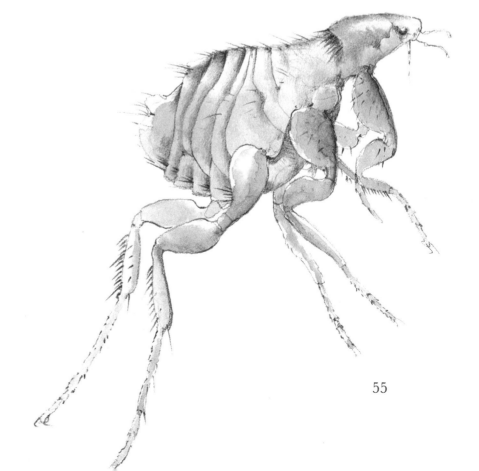

The flea's long legs make it an extraordinary jumper, but it is the insect's lack of wings that allows it to reach such incredible heights. What used to be its wing joints have evolved into a kind of elastic cushion situated behind the joints of its hind legs. When the flea crouches to jump, the hind legs compress these cushions. They rebound rapidly, forcing the hind legs down for their powerful spring.

The Turtle
and the Tortoise

Turtles and their land-dwelling brother tortoises have evolved such highly modified body structures that they resemble no other earthly creature. In their embryonic stages they look a good deal like other reptiles, but their reliance on a shell as a means of defense leads them in a radically different direction as they develop. The inside of their body has been forced to change to accommodate the shell. The shell itself is made of a layer of bony plates covered by a layer of

horny plates. The backbone, fused to the shell plates, is bent into an arch. To support all this weight, the ribs have grown broad and flat, and shoulders and hips have moved into the chest cavity. Since the turtle's body is locked into a rigid case of bone, it cannot breathe as other animals do, by expanding its chest to inflate the lungs. Instead it contracts a set of muscles near its hind legs. This makes room around the lungs, which can then expand to admit air.

56

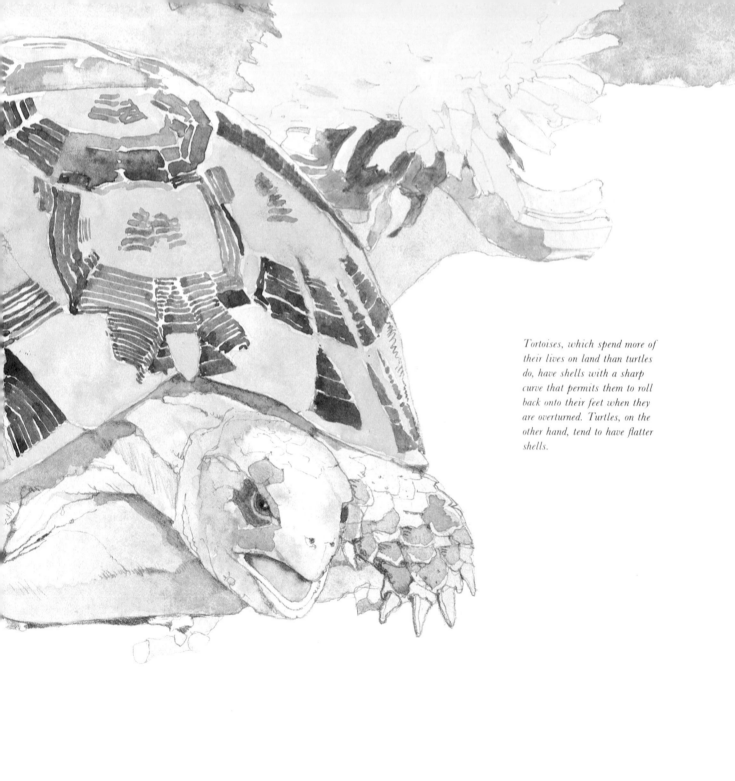

Tortoises, which spend more of their lives on land than turtles do, have shells with a sharp curve that permits them to roll back onto their feet when they are overturned. Turtles, on the other hand, tend to have flatter shells.

A baby turtle hatches by pecking a hole in its shell with a sharpened point on its beak (the same device used by hatching birds) called the egg tooth. As it takes its first breaths, its body expands, gradually cracking the leathery shell, a process that takes about six hours. It then chews a hole in the shell large enough to crawl through.

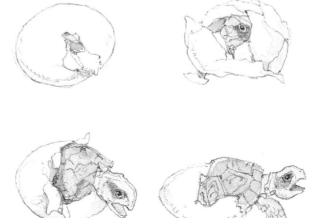

To exhale, the turtle pushes its internal organs against the lungs, forcing the stale air out.

Historically, turtles are among the animals most exploited by man. Most primitive peoples who live where turtles are plentiful eat them. Vast numbers have been slaughtered for the horny plates of their shells, which are heated and removed to make tortoiseshell ornaments and combs. During the nineteenth century, whaling ships stocked up on Galápagos tortoises when they stopped at those Pacific islands during their voyages. The creatures survived well on shipboard, providing a long-term source of fresh meat for the sailors. In this country, diamondback terrapins were an important source of food for slaves on many coastal plantations.

Although most people in this country are not enthusiastic about the meat of reptiles, turtle soup is considered a delicacy. The soup is actually made from a cartilage, called calipee, that lines the lower shell of marine turtles. Turtles continue to be slaughtered just for this cartilage, and the demand is creating a severe drain on several species of sea turtle.

People seem to keep finding new ways to make commercial use of turtles. During the 1960s it became popular to keep turtles as pets. Great Britain alone imported a quarter of a million Greek spur-thighed tortoises for this purpose, which decimated the wild

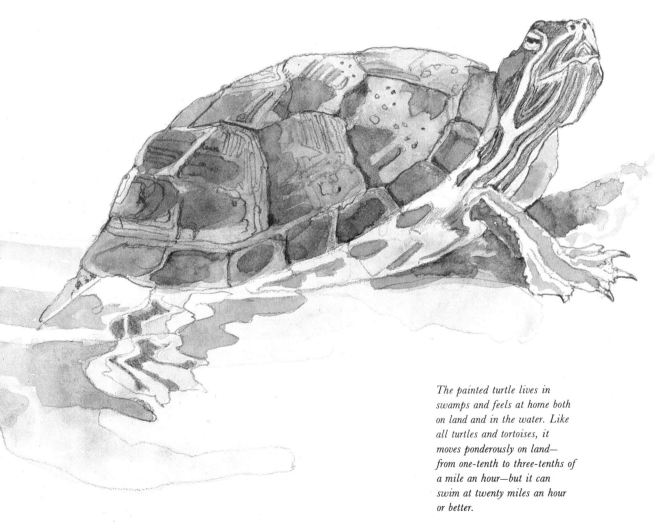

The painted turtle lives in swamps and feels at home both on land and in the water. Like all turtles and tortoises, it moves ponderously on land—from one-tenth to three-tenths of a mile an hour—but it can swim at twenty miles an hour or better.

population. The eastern United States exported hundreds of thousands of red-eared and painted turtles all over the world. Some of these were bred for the purpose on turtle farms, but many were caught in the wild. Unfortunately for most pet turtles, only about 1 percent survive for even one year. Most people who buy them believe they are getting a cute little no-care pet, but this is far from true. Much commercial turtle food is not nutritious enough to sustain life. In addition, turtles require exactly the right conditions of temperature and humidity and just the right amount of ultraviolet light, and they must be kept free of drafts. If the proper environment is provided, and the turtles are fed a properly balanced and varied diet, they can be kept alive in captivity. Most pet turtles, however, spend their captive lives slowly dying.

In their natural habitat, turtles and tortoises thrive, and have been doing so for a long time, for they belong to one of the oldest genera on earth. A very small reptile, with flat ribs and the beginnings of a shell, lived 250 million years ago. It is believed to be the ancestor of modern turtles. Individual turtles are also exceptionally long-lived. Herpetologists believe that they can live to be 100, though few do; most meet with accidents before that. But there are accounts of turtles living even longer. One report, believed to be reliable, says that a giant tortoise killed near Madagascar was 152 years old at death.

The Gull

Black-headed gulls (which actually have brown heads in summer and white heads with a brown patch under the eye in winter) were originally found only in Asia and Europe, but in recent years some have spent their winters in North America.

Dipping and wheeling, cawing plaintively, a flock of gulls is a familiar sight to shore dwellers. Gulls live in close association with people; their huge populations are due mainly to the presence of man and his wastes.

Originally, herring gulls—as the commonest species of "sea gull" is properly known—fed on fish in cold northern waters, mostly small fish that were chased to the surface by large predators such as tuna. The size of

60

houses, dumps, fishing boats and tuna canneries. They follow large ships, ferry boats and small craft, almost anything afloat, looking for a handout. They may be found anywhere there is something to eat. In the course of changing their diet, some gulls have moved inland. Here they find a source of food in rodents, rabbits, ducks and even the eggs of other gulls.

Gulls are social birds, living, breeding and nesting in huge flocks. They have an elaborate system of communication, with at least twenty known calls, each with a different meaning.

One interesting facet of gulls' behavior is controlled by instinct. Researchers noticed that when adult birds returned to their nests, the fledglings would peck at their parents' bills. This pecking caused the adults to regurgitate food they had carried home in their crops. Upon further investigation, the scientists found that the young birds' target was apparently the conspicuous red spot all adult gulls have on their bills. Laboratory experiments using various fake bills confirmed that baby gulls preferred gull-like bills that were long and thin, and also preferred red to any other color.

gull colonies was controlled by the availability of their natural food supply. But herring gulls are supremely adaptable, and they are not picky eaters. Many nowadays make a living from garbage. Where local populations, dependent on a natural food supply, once numbered in the thousands, they now are present in the tens of thousands. Gulls congregate around slaughter-

The herring gull, with its white body and grey mantle, is the best-known gull of North America. It is named after the fish that makes up part of its varied diet. These two are filling up at a garbage dump. Some gulls have been seen carrying clams aloft and purposely dropping them on stones. Having cracked the shells, the gulls can then peck out the tasty insides.

61

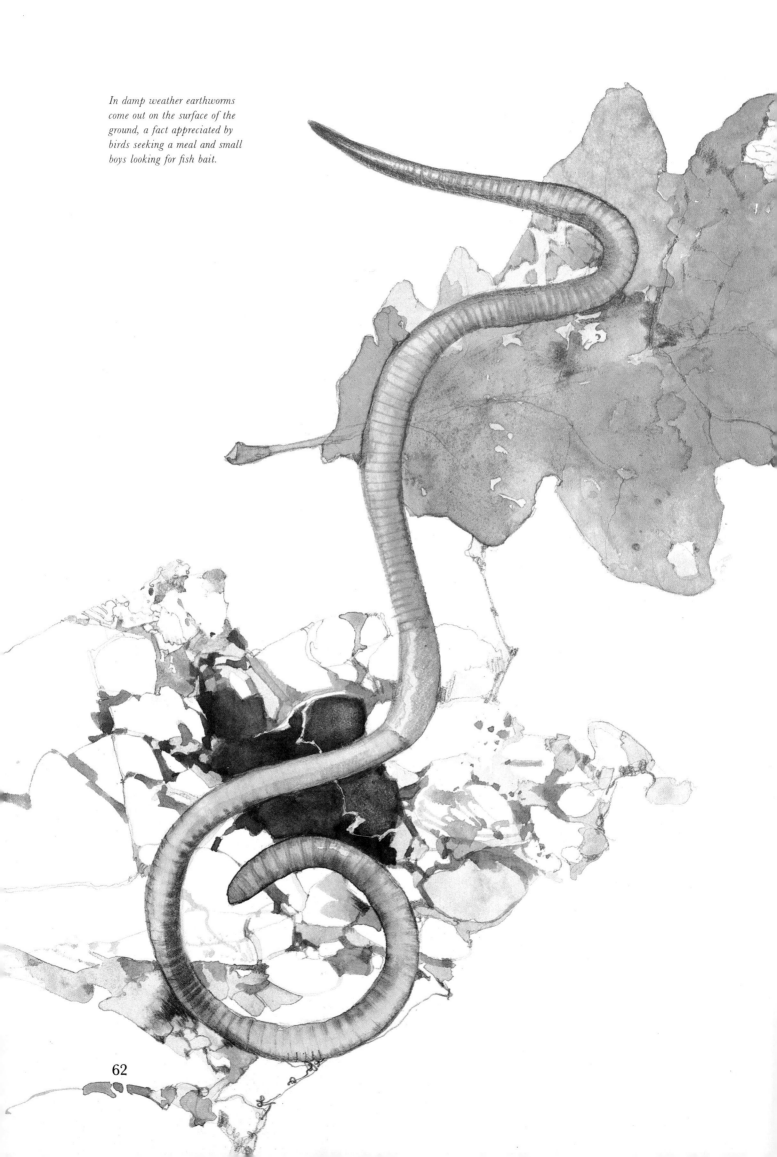

In damp weather earthworms come out on the surface of the ground, a fact appreciated by birds seeking a meal and small boys looking for fish bait.

62

Earthworms have to mate, although each individual contains the organs of both sexes. They do not fertilize themselves, which assures that each new hatch of worms will have a fresh mix of genetic material.

The Earthworm

Many people feel revulsion when they see a worm, but to a gardener every worm is a welcome sight, because earthworms are a sign of a loose and fertile soil. Without worms the soil of our gardens and farmlands would become dense, hard, and difficult to work. Worms spend their lives literally eating dirt, digesting its nutrients, and then passing it out behind them as droppings called castings. These castings are an excellent fertilizer, and the earthworms' tunnels loosen the soil and allow air to penetrate. In a loose soil roots can grow easily, and plants will be strong and healthy. In addition rainwater flows into a loose soil, rather than just washing over the surface. In a single acre of grassland soil there may be three million worms at work, turning over and conditioning some twenty-five tons of soil each year.

Earthworms have been known to perform surprising feats. In one river valley in the Netherlands investigators found a site where a two-foot-thick layer of sand lay over the valley's clay soil. Wondering how it came to be there, they began digging and discovered the remains of an early human habitation. Evidently earthworms had been attracted to the settlement's compost and refuse, and had moved the sand up from beneath the clay layer in the course of their eating and tunneling.

Earthworms move by stretching and shortening their segmented bodies. Each segment has bristles that point backward and keep that segment from slipping back while the segments ahead are stretching forward. The segments start contracting at the front of the worm and the contraction spreads backward, segment by segment, along the worm's body, like a wave. Researchers have found that when one segment contracts, it stretches the one behind it, stimulating it to contract in its turn. Thus the wave of contraction spreads along the worm automatically. The worm's contractions are independent of its central nervous system. Even if those nerves are severed, the segments continue their contractions.

Like many simple animals, earthworms can regenerate lost parts, and even a head can be created anew. If a worm is cut in half it does not die, but grows into two complete new worms.

63

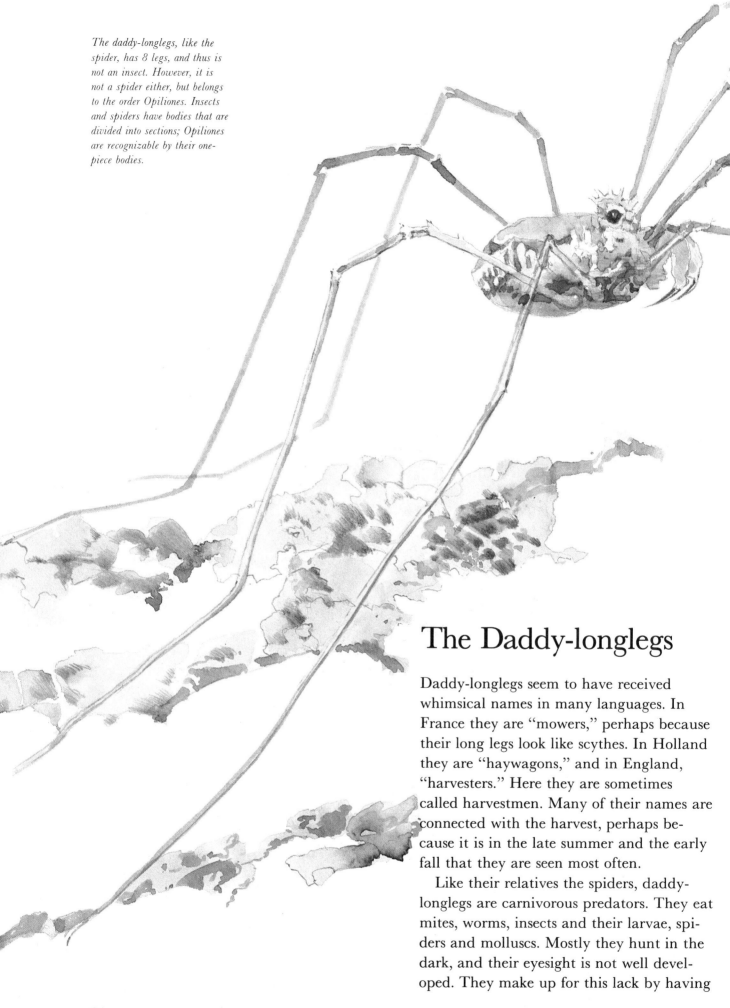

The Daddy-longlegs

Daddy-longlegs seem to have received whimsical names in many languages. In France they are "mowers," perhaps because their long legs look like scythes. In Holland they are "haywagons," and in England, "harvesters." Here they are sometimes called harvestmen. Many of their names are connected with the harvest, perhaps because it is in the late summer and the early fall that they are seen most often.

Like their relatives the spiders, daddy-longlegs are carnivorous predators. They eat mites, worms, insects and their larvae, spiders and molluscs. Mostly they hunt in the dark, and their eyesight is not well developed. They make up for this lack by having

64

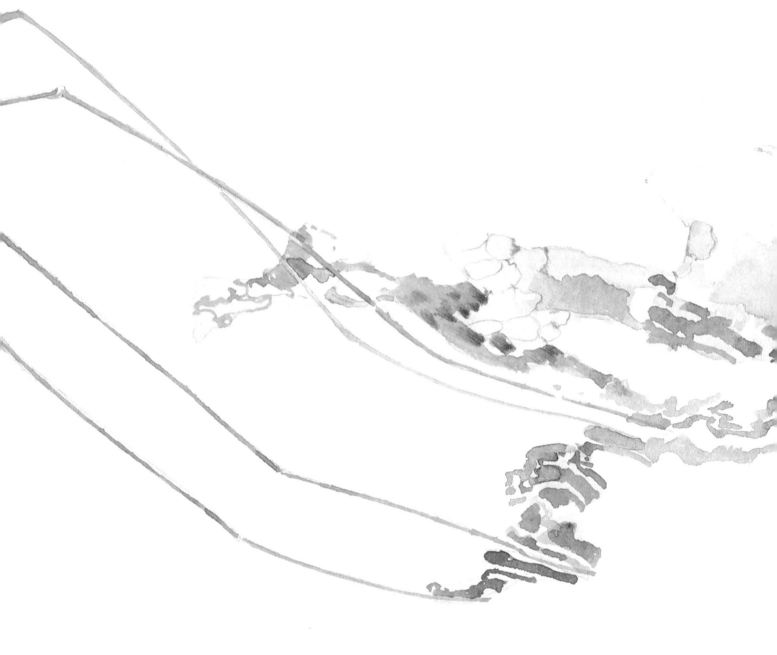

organs of smell in their legs, which help them to locate their prey.

Daddy-longlegs have several methods of escaping from being preyed upon themselves. If their long legs do not carry them away fast enough, they have a pair of glands that squirt out a foul-smelling substance irritating to predators. Some species can squirt it ten inches, stopping an attack before it gets started. If the repellent does not work, the daddy-longlegs is capable of shedding his legs when they are seized. Each leg has weak spots where it will break off easily. The predator is left holding a leg, which distracts his attention by twitching for a while after it comes loose. The daddy-longlegs makes his escape on his other legs, and is quite capable of surviving with more than one missing.

Different species of daddy-longlegs are adapted to a wide range of different environments. Not all of the species have such delicate long legs as the common ones we are used to seeing. In cold climates they often hibernate together in groups. A mass of seventy thousand daddy-longlegs were found hibernating together inside a giant cactus in Mexico.

The Dog

A Great Dane's benign expression reflects the transformation of a once wild animal, through eons of domestication and selective breeding, into a true friend of man.

There is probably no animal more completely domesticated than the dog. Bred into almost every possible shape and size, suited for purposes as different as hunting badgers (the dachshund) and rescuing stranded mountain travelers (the St. Bernard), the dog thoroughly and utterly belongs to man. A tomcat will wander off into the woods and stay all summer, a mother cat will move her kittens to the neighbor's house if they have better food or a warmer spot by the fire. But even a hungry, ill-treated dog will stick with his master.

What is it about the psychological

makeup of dogs that make them fit so easily into the lifestyle of humans? Dogs, after all, are not slaves, confined like horses and cattle and forced to serve. They do not have to be kept; they stay because they want to.

Konrad Lorenz, the famed Austrian naturalist, and one of the founding fathers of the science of animal behavior, has thought and written extensively on this subject. In one of his books, *King Solomon's Ring,* he postulates that there have been two separate pathways to domesticity in modern dogs. He believes that the first type of doglike creature to follow man was the jackal. In northwestern Europe the bones of a partially domesticated jackallike dog have been found in association with those of Stone Age man. Jackals presumably followed hunters to get scraps from their kills, and gradually learned not only to follow but to assist the hunters by tracking and bringing their game to bay.

In the long process of domestication men selected and bred dogs that retained some of their juvenile characteristics into adulthood. These features, such as a domed skull, a short nose and hanging ears appeal to people's instincts. The dogs also retained a strong love for their mothers, which they transferred, as they grew up, into an adoration of people. Dogs like shepherds, spaniels, retrievers and pointers show these characteristics strongly. This type of dog tends to love everybody and is constantly either lavishing licks and tail-wagging on his master or cringing at his feet like a frightened pup.

The other line of descent in modern dogs stems from the wolf. This blood is a much later addition and exists in its purest form in sled dogs like the malamute, husky and samoyed. These dogs look different and act much differently from the jackal-type dogs. They share with their wolf ancestors high cheekbones, slanted eyes and upwardly tilted noses. These are the "one-man dogs" that attach themselves to one master at the age of 6 to 8 months, and accept orders

Terrier puppies growl fiercely and wag their tails in an attack on a red rubber ball.

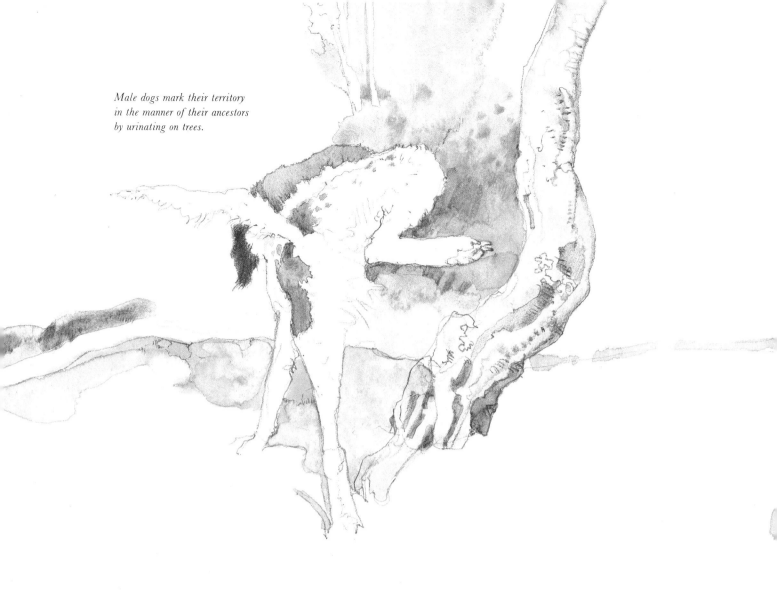

from no other. Their loyalty comes from the wolf's natural allegiance to his pack leader, and his almost human degree of regard for members of his pack. Dogs with a great deal of wolf blood are dignified and do not cringe or fawn or throw themselves into the laps of their human masters like jackal-type dogs. On the other hand, the wolf-types are not nearly so obedient or eager to please. Most modern dogs display a mixture of traits from both these ancestors.

One trait that almost all dogs share is a highly developed sense of smell. A dog has seventy square inches of mucous membrane lining its nose, compared to less than one square inch in man, and the dog's smelling acuity is correspondingly greater. For this

reason St. Bernards can track lost mountaineers buried in the snow, while hounds can follow the trail a fox has made hours before.

Even this acute sense of smell does not explain how dogs can perform miraculous feats of finding their way home. There are many marvelous stories of lost dogs returned, but one of the most amazing has to be that of a tiny fox terrier who lost his master and crossed more than sixteen hundred miles of the Australian continent, traveling for eight months, before he reached home, still, of course, wagging his tail. How did he do it? There are still many unanswered questions about our companion from before the dawn of history.

Dogs show submission by cringing, flattening themselves on the ground and tucking their tails between their legs.

A chained dog snarls at an intruder. He is all the more ferocious because of being chained and unable either to escape or to defend his territory properly. He would be much less aggressive were he left off his chain.

69

Jersey cows are smaller than Holsteins, and although they produce less milk, it is creamier than Holstein milk. Many farmers prefer Jerseys because they are gentle and easy to handle.

Black and white Holstein cows originally came to North America from Holland, and are the highest-producing and most popular breed of cow on modern dairy farms.

The Cow

The dairy cow is one of modern agriculture's most successful creations. A big black and white Holstein cow will give twenty times her own weight in milk in a year— that is, ten thousand quarts or even more. At the same time she maintains her own body, providing six hundred pounds of beef at the end of her milking life, and bears a calf a year as well.

Cows are extremely efficient converters of rough, indigestible feed, such as grass and grain by-products, into human food. Their efficiency comes from the fact that they are ruminants, a class of animals with complex stomachs. A cow's stomach is divided into four parts. As she grazes she stuffs grass into herself as fast as she can, without chewing it. The feed goes into her rumen, a huge sac that holds sixty gallons of food and fluid. After she has eaten her fill, she looks for a shady spot to lie down, and starts chewing her cud, or ruminating. She burps up a mouthful of the previously swallowed grass and starts to chew it, so that it will be easier to digest. She then swallows it back down to the rumen, which houses a vast population of bacteria and protozoa. These microorganisms have the ability to break down and digest cellulose, the tough outer covering of plant cells. Without these "bugs" the cow could digest grass no better than we can. Once chewed and back in the rumen, the food passes along through three more stomach chambers, where both the original grass and the rumen organisms that helped digest it are further digested. This process allows the cow to extract energy, and thus make milk, from parts of the plant that would otherwise be wasted.

Inky black from the tip of its beak to the end of its tail, a crow flaps its way aloft.

Two ravens fly in circles, rising on currents of warm air.

72

The Crow

The sight of a couple of big black crows flapping away from the smashed remains of a road-killed rabbit or squirrel does not fill most people with affection for the birds. Yet carrion must be disposed of, and crows, who help rid the world of carcasses, are actually interesting and likeable birds.

Members of the crow family, which also includes ravens, jays and magpies, are the most intelligent of all birds. They can learn to count and have an extensive language of calls. Most of their sounds are *caws,* but they can also make a musical warble. Some observers claim that crows will care for and feed an old or injured member of their species. The birds make good pets and can be taught to speak words like a parrot. If a young crow is taken from its nest before it is two weeks old it will accept a human as its parent, and follow him around, ignoring other crows. It is not necessary to keep such a civilized crow in a cage, for it will always return to the house in which it is raised.

Crows are most common in the eastern United States, although there are large local populations in the West. Canadian crows and those from our northern states usually migrate south for the winter, and may gather into huge flocks. In the 1920s two hundred thousand crows roosted near Washington, D.C. When such a number gather in one place the birds may have to fly fifty miles to feed, but nevertheless return each night to their communal roost.

The largest member of the crow family is the raven, which is common in the far North and the West. It has a wingspread of over 4 feet and is an exceptionally strong flyer. It flies like a hawk, rising and circling, and can stay aloft even in a gale. Like the crow it is intelligent and wary; it prefers wilderness areas, and does not associate as closely with man as does its more adaptable cousin.

The Cardinal, the Blue Jay and the Chickadee

Three of the most familiar birds at a bird feeder in the eastern United States are chickadees, blue jays and cardinals. Blue jays can't be mistaken—there is no other large blue bird with a crested head. They are also bold, aggressive birds at the feeder, and so are very easy to spot.

Winter seems to bring out the noise in jays. They have a variety of calls, from *jay, jay* to *kuk, kuk, kuk*, as well as growls and musical notes. They also have a song of low notes and whistles, which they sing only when they are well hidden. Very few people

Blue jays have a well-deserved reputation as thieves. Here one steals an egg from a pair of cardinals.

Hanging upside down, a mother chickadee feeds her nestlings, which have grown big enough to perch on a branch outside their nest.

ever get to hear it. At mating times the birds become quiet, perhaps so they will not give away the location of their nest.

The cardinal, as red as the jay is blue, becomes quite tame around houses equipped with bird feeders. Often two or three pairs will stay close by for the entire winter. The females are much duller colored than the brilliant red males, with red only on the wings, tail, crest and bill. Their bodies are olive green.

The female cardinal chooses the nesting site, and builds there a nest of twigs and grass, lined with hair or soft grasses. She incubates her eggs, while her mate brings her food. When the eggs hatch, both parents feed the babies. The male may take sole charge of them when they first learn to fly, while the female nests again with a second clutch of eggs.

Chickadees are many people's favorite bird to feed because they become very tame. Often they will learn to land on an outstretched hand if rewarded every time with a sunflower seed. Chickadees get their name from their call: *chicka deee dee dee dee.* Usually they make one or two *chickas* and four or more *dees;* sometimes they leave out the *chicka* altogether. Both males and females also sing a *PHEE-bee, PHEE-bee* song, especially in the spring. The sound of the first *PHEE-bee* is a good sign that spring is on the way.

In the winter chickadees live in the wild in flocks with populations of around thirty birds per hundred acres. In spring the flocks disperse, breaking up into pairs, with each male defending a territory that can extend up to seventeen acres. The female builds a nest and lays between 5 and 8 eggs, but usually 7, and while she sits on them her mate feeds her. When the eggs hatch, both parents feed the young. The work of feeding the hatchlings is so exhausting that the parents can live for only sixteen hours without food for themselves.

75

The Magpie

Magpies are members of the crow family, and are a common bird in our western states. Occasionally specimens wander into the eastern part of the country, but for the most part they stay west of the Mississippi.

Like crows, magpies are among our most intelligent birds. Their call is a raucous shriek. They do not seem to be popular birds, and in Europe they are regarded as harbingers of death. They are certainly intelligent enough to be good at stealing, often filching eggs from chicken houses, sometimes even taking young chicks. However, they make up for their thievery by eating mice, snails, rats and snakes. They even land on the backs of sheep and cattle

Bright black and white markings make the magpie an easy bird to identify.

76

A magpie carries off a twig, which it will use to build its nest.

in order to eat the ticks they find there. Probably, all things considered, magpies do us as much good as harm.

Magpies build their nests high in trees, nests as heavily armored and hard to penetrate as a fortress. The birds weave together twigs, branches, hay and hair, and then cement it all together with mud. The resulting mess makes a covering so strong that even a hunter's shot cannot go through it.

Magpies have another defense against hunters in their peculiar, fluttering way of flying. Since their flight pattern is so erratic, they make a difficult target for both human and animal predators. It is not certain why they developed this peculiar habit. It may be that their long, forked tail makes straight and level flight difficult, or it may be just the path evolution has chosen to protect the species.

The Raccoon

The sound of a crashing garbage can at dusk means but one thing to suburban and country people—raccoons are at the garbage again, and strong springs and tightly fitted lids have posed no problem for their skillful "hands."

Raccoons are one of a number of adaptable animals that have fitted themselves into a way of life based partly on human refuse. They are willing to eat almost anything: vegetables, meat, insects, berries, grain or garbage—whatever is available. Human civilization provides them with many of their needs. Gardens offer sweet corn and berries, two of their favorites. Most gardeners have to build elaborate fences, often electrified, to keep the coons from harvesting their corn. For some reason

A suburban raccoon gnaws on a bone after deftly turning over a garbage pail.

78

Captive raccoons always wash their food before eating it, perhaps to remove some scent or grit from it. Wild raccoons have been seen washing their food, too, but they seem to do it less consistently than tame ones.

the animals always seem to raid the garden just the day before the corn is ripe, pulling down every stalk, taking random bites from all the ears, and leaving none to be harvested by those who carefully tended it all summer. Chicken is another raccoon favorite, and many a farmer has come out to feed his fowl at dawn only to discover a hole in the fence and several hens fewer than he had the night before.

Raccoons can be fierce fighters, and are a match for almost any dog. They have a frighteningly loud growl, and they puff out their hair to make themselves look huge and dangerous in a fight. Often coon hounds come home from a night hunt half blinded or missing an ear.

Despite their ferocity in the wild, raccoons can make good pets. Nothing is more irresistible than a baby raccoon with its almost human hands and its masked little face. Although a raccoon's behavior can grow somewhat unpredictable as it ages, it does not necessarily turn mean; many people have kept raccoons successfully for years.

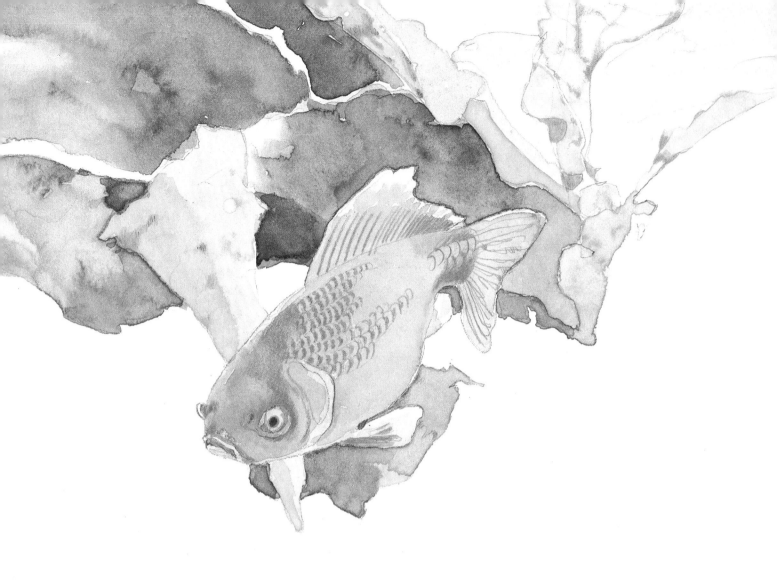

The Goldfish

Goldfish, because of their many virtues, certainly rank as one of the world's most popular pets. They are clean, cheap to feed, take up very little space and respond to the attentions of their human keepers. In addition, they can endure less-than-perfect care without dying.

All of the modern strains of goldfish are descended from a plain little brown fish called the Johnny carp. They are closely related to, and can interbreed with, the common carp, which originated near the Black and Caspian seas, but now has been introduced to temperate waters all over the world. Carp grow fast and are an important source of protein in many places.

Much of the selective breeding of goldfish has been done in Japan. There, breeders have created a vast array of different strains. There are goldfish with huge bug

eyes, bulging heads, arched backs and drooping tails. Some of these fish are so distorted they can hardly swim, but some fish fanciers find them beautiful. Others have lost their natural hardiness, and have to live out their artificial lives in a state of ungoldfishlike delicate health.

One of the reasons goldfish are so easy to keep in home aquariums lies in their habit of rising to the surface to gulp air. Although they cannot depend totally on this method of breathing, the air they take in through their mouths can supplement the dissolved oxygen they breathe in through their gills. Aquariums, especially those that lack green plants or air-pumping apparatus, may have insufficient oxygen dissolved in the water to support most fish. Those that cannot breathe through their mouths as well as their gills will die under such circumstances.

80

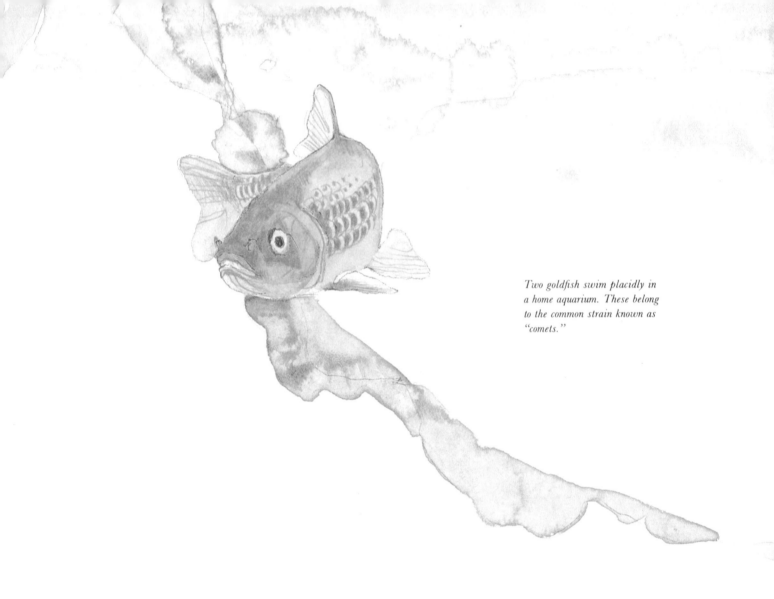

Two goldfish swim placidly in a home aquarium. These belong to the common strain known as "comets."

Not all goldfish live in indoor tanks. They also do well in ponds, outdoor fountains, and the like, where they grow into big fish. Goldfish adjust their size to their surroundings: in a small bowl inside they will limit their size to a few inches—but outdoors in a large pool they may grow to be a foot long.

Their habit of coming to the surface for food and air occasionally leads to a strange behavior pattern: a bird may stop at the edge of a pond and stuff a worm into a fish's gaping mouth. It doesn't take the fish long to learn to come to the surface to beg.

A mother bird feeds a goldfish, perhaps mistaking it for one of her nestlings. Animal behaviorists call this kind of aberrant behavior "misfiring": the bird's behavior is correct but directed to the wrong object.

Birds that feed fish in this manner may have lost their own babies and need to satisfy their strong desire to stuff food into an open mouth.

81

The Snail

Snails are molluscs, a group of soft-bodied invertebrates with protective shells. They are close relatives of clams, mussels and squid. Snails are the commonest class of molluscs; there are more than seventy thousand living species.

Human interest in snails has a long history, partly because they are delicious. In Europe, and to some extent in this country, snails served with garlic, butter and herbs are considered to be a gourmet dish. The meat of snails has long been thought to have healing properties. In the first century A.D. Pliny the Elder described a variety of diseases that could be cured by eating snails, or certain parts of their shells.

Ground-up snail shells placed in a hollow tooth were supposed to relieve diarrhea, as well as various swellings. Other reports claimed that tuberculosis could be helped by eating snail meat, and that warts could be dried up by rubbing them with a snail and then sticking the poor snail on a thorn until it dried up. Not all snail remedies have turned out to be mere superstition. In parts of Europe country people used to treat asthma, bronchitis and whooping cough by feeding the patient cooked snails. Nobody understood why this remedy worked until it was discovered that some snails excrete antibacterial substances.

In tropical parts of the world, however,

snails play a darker part in man's life. Some
species are the intermediate host to a small
parasitic worm called the schistosome.
These worms travel through the human cir-
culatory system, damaging blood vessels as
they go, then lay their eggs in the lower in-
testine. Discharged with human wastes, the
eggs hatch into swimming embryos, which
seek out a snail. Once inside the snail they
multiply, then metamorphose into larvae.
The snail has served its purpose and the larvae leave to find a human host, whom they
enter through the skin. They wriggle their
way to the bloodstream, where they mate
and lay their eggs. Thus the cycle begins
again. The disease, schistosomiasis, is pain-

*Two mating snails press their
"feet" together. These snails
are bisexual and each passes
genetic material to the other.*

ful and sometimes fatal, and infects around 100 million people worldwide.

A snail's body is made up of three main parts. It has a head, with a mouth and two sensitive antennae, a muscular foot, which supports the body, and a fold of skin on the back called the mantle. A snail moves on its foot by first laying down a layer of mucus. The muscles of the foot then undergo wave-like contractions that slide the snail along its slimy path. The function of the mantle is to secrete the shell. It has a tiny network of tubes that excrete little specks of limestone.

The grove snail is one of many species with highly decorated shells. Special pigment-secreting glands spaced at intervals along the edge of the mantle lay down the colored stripes as the shell is formed.

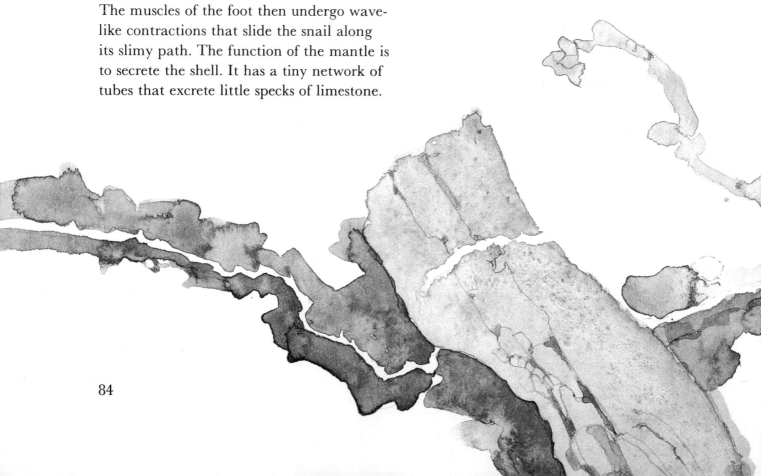

The specks are cemented together with a hornlike substance to form the shell.

Snail species live in a vast range of different environments, and in most of them it is their shell that allows them to survive. In times of drought snails can draw into their shells and close up the entrance with a layer of slime to prevent themselves from drying up. One snail lived this way for six years, taped to a shelf in a British museum. Desert-living snails have a further modification in having white shells that reflect the light of the sun, to prevent the shell from acting like a solar collector and roasting the snail inside.

Some kinds of mollusc lack shells in their adult forms, though they have them in their larval stages. One such animal is the slug, a kind of shell-less snail. Vegetable gardeners are familiar with these pests, which are often found clinging to the bottom of lettuce leaves, or deep inside the florets of a cauliflower. As is the case with many members of the snail family, both sexes are present in each individual of the great grey slug. In this species courtship takes place on a high tree or wall. The partners drop down on a foot-long thread of slime to exchange their seed. It is hard to believe that such simple creatures, which look to us like mere blobs of flesh, and which are known to have an extremely simple nervous system, are nonetheless capable of intricately patterned behavior.

Slugs and snails can move over sharp objects such as these rocks, or even the edge of a razor blade, without cutting their soft bodies, because they secrete a protective layer of slime that acts like a cushion. Left behind, it is the familiar "snail trail."

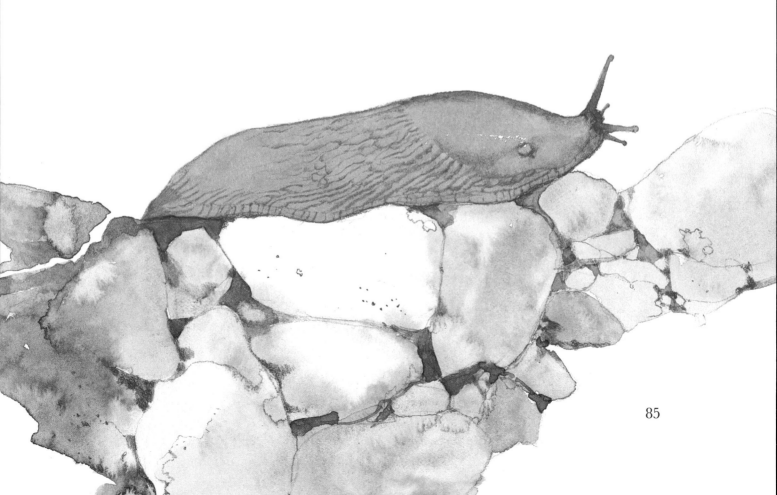

The Guinea Pig

While most of the rodents that live on intimate terms with man, such as rats and mice, are a nuisance and a health hazard, the guinea pig has done us nothing but good. These little rodents are used extensively in laboratory experiments and many of us probably owe our lives to those sacrificed in the course of medical research. In addition, of course, guinea pigs make pleasant pets.

Domestic guinea pigs, shown about life size above, have been bred to produce coats of many colors and textures. Babies raised in captivity, like the ones at left, grow into quiet, clean and gentle pets.

Cavies, as guinea pigs are also called, live wild in South America, from Colombia to the top of Argentina. The wild ones look more like rats than do the domesticated ones. They have sharper noses, more streamlined bodies and rough brown or grey hair. Like many domestic species, adult domesticated guinea pigs retain some juvenile characteristics: they have smooth hair, rounded heads and plump bodies.

Ancient Incas kept guinea pigs both as a source of meat and for sacrifices to the gods. When the Spanish conquerors came to America, they found not only gold but guinea pigs. However, it was Dutch explorers, rather than the Spanish, who introduced the animal to Europe in the middle of the sixteenth century.

Guinea pigs are easy to raise in captivity, although they are nervous animals (a mother may kill and eat her babies if she is disturbed or frightened when they are still very young). Usually she has a litter of 3 or 4 after a gestation period of about 2 months. The young nurse for 3 weeks, maturing and becoming capable of reproduction themselves when they are only about 2 months old.

The Fly

Flies live everywhere. There are species of Diptera, the group that includes flies, mosquitoes and gnats, adapted to every climate on earth. Flies are responsible for spreading a vast number of diseases, mainly because of their method of feeding.

The housefly has no mouth parts for biting hard objects or puncturing skin, so it eats by lapping or sponging up its food. It favors rotting organic material, such as garbage, sewage and other materials that are laden with the organisms of disease. When a fly that has recently fed on sewage gets into the house and settles on a plate of meat or a nice sticky cake, it spits out a drop of its stomach contents to moisten this new food source. Although it laps most of

this drop up again, it still leaves behind millions of bacteria or viruses to infect the person for whom the food was intended. Even if the fly only walks on the food, it leaves organisms and bits of material behind, because it has hairy legs that tend to catch and trap particles of the rotten materials that it favors.

Although flies are harmful and annoying, they are also quite interesting. A fly placidly walking upside down along the ceiling, or straight up the slippery vertical face of a window pane, seems to defy the laws of physics. However, close inspection of the structure of its legs reveals how the insect can perform these feats. Each leg ends in two claws with a pad between them. If

A fly lands upside down on a ceiling by doing a lightning-fast somersault. When it flies it holds its front legs forward and up. As soon as it feels its legs touch the ceiling, it flips over.

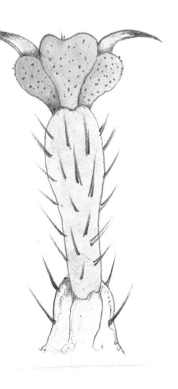

Examined through a microscope, a fly's foot shows its two ways of clinging to surfaces. On a rough surface, the fly employs tiny claws. On a smooth surface, such as glass, the pinkish suction cups come into play, exuding a bit of liquid that makes the suction more efficient.

there is any roughness or irregularity to the surface, the fly holds on to it with its claws. On a smooth surface the fly makes use of tiny hollow hairs on its pads. These secrete a liquid made by special glands. The surface tension of this liquid permits the fly to adhere to the surface.

One of the reasons for the world's great abundance of flies lies in the insect's rapid reproductive rate. A female fly lives for about 2 months, and during this time she lays about 1,000 eggs. If all of her offspring lived, and all of their offspring lived, one fly, in the course of a 5-month breeding season, could populate the area with 5.5 billion flies.

A winter wren, its tail cocked up at a typically wren-like angle, sings from its perch on a chicken-wire fence. At right a house wren builds one of his several nests of the season in an old shoe.

The Wren

Wrens are small, brown, perky birds that can be recognized by the upward slant of their tails and their downwardly curving bills. A variety of wrens occupy different habitats in the United States.

The winter wren is one of America's smallest songbirds. It may have taken its name from the fact that a few individuals fail to migrate, and winter-over in southern Canada and the northern United States. Most, however, fly south for the winter. In the summers, these wrens live in the cool pinewoods and swamps where there is little direct sunshine. They eat almost nothing but insects—bark beetles, wood borers, aphids, moths, and the like. They tend to stay fairly close to the ground, nesting in the roots of fallen trees or under a peeling layer of bark on a dead tree. They build their nests out of twigs, grass, and moss and line them with hair and feathers. The males of this species, like those of other wrens, are great nest builders. So enthusiastic are they that they may make four or more extra nests, which are never used.

House wrens are a little larger and a bit paler-colored than winter wrens. Why they are called house wrens is not certain; perhaps because they will make their nests in birdhouses or in the cracks and crevices of human habitations. House wrens prefer a much more open habitat than winter wrens. They live along the edges of woods and in yards and gardens around houses. Male house wrens build several nests in such places as abandoned hornets' nests or woodpecker holes, or even in the eye sockets of an old cow skull left lying in a pasture. The female will investigate all of the prospective nesting sites before choosing one to lay her eggs in. She lines the one she has chosen with hair or soft feathers, cocoons or catkins. Both parents care for the babies, and are so solicitous that they will even feed young birds of other species. On the other hand, if the local wren population gets too high, the males will destroy eggs and even kill young wrens.

90

The Centipede
and the Millipede

Centipedes and millipedes are small worm-shaped creatures that, being arthropods, are related to crabs and lobsters. Their names imply that they have a hundred, or a thousand, legs. They do have a great many legs, but not that many.

Both animals have bodies made up of a large number of segments. Centipedes can have up to 15 such segments, with 1 pair of legs per segment, for a total of 30. Millipedes, not surprisingly, have more segments—as many as 50—and have 2 pairs of legs on each segment, so may have 200 legs.

Centipedes can be dangerous creatures, as one researcher in Africa found. In the course of her study of tropical species of the many-legged creatures, she found no shortage of specimens, and collected them in a

A centipede hunts its prey by feeling for it with its antennae. For most practical purposes, it lacks the senses of both sight and smell.

Millipedes have so many legs that they have to move them in careful sequence lest they get tangled. Each leg swings out and forward, then back and down in turn, to stay out of the way of its neighbors.

plastic bag. She soon began feeling tired and dizzy, and noticed that each time she opened the bag to add a new centipede she felt worse. Then she saw that all her specimens were dying. It turned out that they were poisoning each other by secreting prussic acid, their natural method of defense. She had come close to being poisoned herself. Prussic acid is a strong poison: only one-twentieth of a gram, if ingested, will kill a human being.

Tropical centipedes are not the only ones that can secrete this poison. The ones living in temperate zones also use it to kill their prey. Centipedes are carnivores, feeding on larvae, insects and the like.

Millipedes, on the other hand, are largely vegetarians. They eat mostly rotting leaves and sometimes the carcasses of animals. Thus they help to turn all such materials into compost, which enriches the soil.

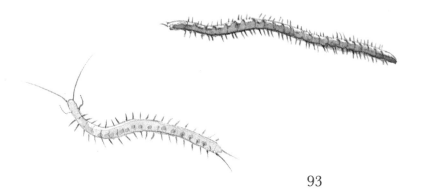

Big ears and small eyes are the trademark of the bat. Most bats hang upside down when they sleep (right). From this position they can simply let go and fall into flight.

The Bat

There are a greater number of species of bat than there are of any other kind of mammal except rodents. Most of them eat mainly insects, fruit or a mixture of both. There are also bats that, like bees, feed on the nectar and pollen of flowers, and there are carnivorous species that eat small animals and fish. There are two species of vampire bat—the bat that lives on blood. Considering the tiny part of the total bat population that these two groups make up, they have given bats as a whole an undeservedly bad name. Where rabies exists in wild populations of rodents such as squirrels, as it does in some parts of the country, bats also can contract the disease. When the virus invades their brains, bats may turn aggressive, and attack and bite people. Mostly, however, humans have little to fear from bats, and in fact some people have found them to be interesting pets.

Most species of bat hunt at night, or at dusk. To find their prey, and to avoid bumping into obstacles in flight, they use a system of echolocation. A hunting bat constantly emits high-pitched sounds, then listens for the echoes. These echoes indicate the distance, and probably the shape, size and consistency of objects in the area. Grown people, who usually lose the ability to hear such high-frequency sounds, cannot detect the bats' squeaks, but young children, whose ears are more sensitive, often say they can hear the bats' "sonar."

Bats catch insects by flying at them with open mouths. If they miss, they scoop the bug up with their wings (left, below).

Bats are the only mammals capable of true flight, although flying squirrels and a few others can glide. Bats' wings are actually highly modified front legs in which the bones of the fingers have grown as long as the bat's whole body. These fingers spread out like spokes to support the membranes of the wings. The membranes contain no flesh at all, but are made of two layers of skin, one from the back and one from the belly, with just enough connective tissue to support the nerves and blood vessels.

During the day bats usually sleep in a dim protected place like a church steeple, behind the shutters of a house, in the high, dark corners of barns, or in a cave or a hollow tree. While they sleep, bats save energy by becoming torpid and allowing their temperature to fall. In winter some species hibernate, reducing their body temperature as much as a hundred times below the normal level. Other species migrate long distances to climates where food is available all winter.

Bats usually have only 1 baby a year. They make up for this low reproductive rate by living for a long time. Some pet bats have been known to live to be 17 years old, although it is unlikely that wild ones can escape death for so long.

Some species of hibernating bats mate in the fall, even though the female does not ovulate until the spring. She stores the male's sperm in her body all winter, and conceives only when the weather warms up. When her young bat is born it climbs up her body and clings to a teat, and for the first two weeks of its life it goes everywhere with its mother, assured of a meal whenever it likes.

The Ladybug

One insect that does man a great deal of good, and no harm, is the ladybug. It seems dedicated to ridding the world of aphids. Both larvae and mature ladybugs eat aphids, as well as other pests such as the corn earworm and the cotton leafworm.

One ladybug (or ladybird beetle, as it is also called) can eat up to sixty aphids a day, ridding crops of harmful pests without endangering the environment, as chemical sprays do. Besides their prodigious appetites ladybugs have another attribute that recommends them to us. In winter ladybugs hibernate, and they tend to do it in large groups. Heaps of garbage or sheltered spots by a house or barn may hide piles containing thousands of ladybugs. In western states and in Europe and Asia ladybugs migrate at hibernation time. In the West they fly from valleys up to the mountains and stay dormant on bushes until spring. So great are their congregations in winter that they can be collected and packed into gallon jars for sale. As long as they are kept cold and dormant they come to no harm, and may be shipped to gardeners and farmers who use them to protect their crops from sucking insects. There are also commercial ladybug breeders who raise the beetles specifically for sale. Some gardeners keep cans of ladybugs in the refrigerator so they can release them in the garden whenever it comes under attack from aphids.

Occasionally huge swarms of ladybugs invade a small area. In England in 1869 the streets of London crawled with ladybugs, and once, near Alexandria, Egypt, there was a swarm of from four to five billion. No one knows what causes these huge populations, but they seem to come at hibernation time.

A ladybug lays her eggs on a flowering rose bush infested with aphids. In this way she assures that as soon as her young hatch, in about 3 weeks, they can have something to eat.

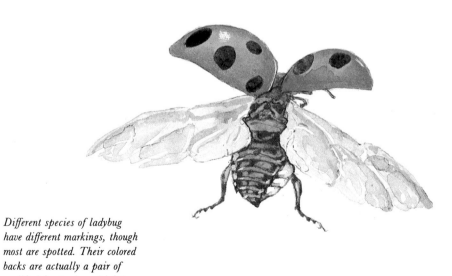

Different species of ladybug have different markings, though most are spotted. Their colored backs are actually a pair of modified front wings (right), which fold down over their backs to form a shield.

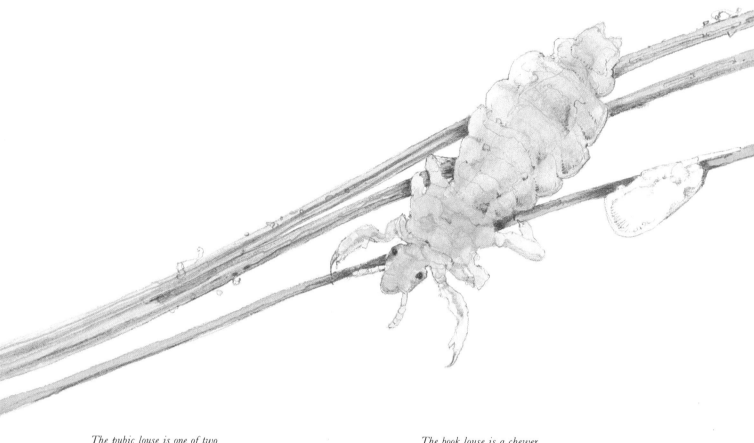

The pubic louse is one of two species that infest man. This one lives in armpits and eyebrows, as well as in the pubic hair. The other species, the head louse, inhabits the head, hair and clothes.

The book louse is a chewer rather than a blood sucker. It lives on the glue of book bindings, and can do extensive damage in libraries.

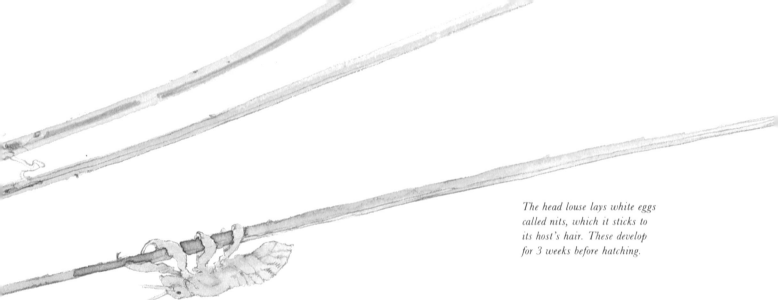

The head louse lays white eggs called nits, which it sticks to its host's hair. These develop for 3 weeks before hatching.

The Louse

The louse ranks as one of mankind's closest and least desirable companions. It has claimed millions of lives in the course of history. Napoleon's armies were decimated during his Russian campaign by typhus, which was spread largely by lice. During the Russian revolution, between 1918 and 1923, louse-spread typhus killed three million soldiers, and still more died from it in both world wars.

Lice feed on human blood by pushing three sharp tubes, called stylets, through the skin. They inject saliva to keep the blood from clotting, and then suck blood into their stomachs. Their bite is irritating, and causes severe itching.

A female louse lays 80 to 100 eggs over the course of about 2 weeks. These eggs, or nits, develop when the temperature is right. Below 68° F they stop developing. They begin again when it is warmer. Once hatched, young lice mature quickly, and within 3 weeks they are ready to lay eggs of their own.

Under poor sanitary conditions people can be infested with thousands of lice. Most people consider lice a sign of neglect and poor hygiene, but there have been times when lice enhanced a person's reputation. In the Middle Ages, the more lice found on a saint the more he was venerated. When the English archbishop Thomas à Becket was murdered in 1170, his clothes were described as "boiling over like a pot of water on the fire" with lice. Shortly thereafter he was canonized.

Today lice can be controlled by observing good sanitation and hygiene, and by killing the lice with insecticides when they do appear. However, for reasons that are not entirely understood, head lice seem to be staging a comeback, especially in schools. Since lice can move easily from head to head under crowded conditions, and thrive in a population that shares its combs, scarves, hats and coats in the indiscriminate way of schoolchildren, it may be that infestations of lice will be an unwelcome but common feature of modern life, as they have been throughout the course of human history.

A fancy-feathered cock crows from the top of a barnyard manure pile while two of his harem of hens peck for bugs and grain at his feet.

The Chicken

No other kind of animal has lived longer and in closer association with man than the chicken. In the fourth century B.C., one Eastern philosopher wrote that he had learned four things from the cock: to fight, to get up early, to eat with your family and to protect your spouse when she gets into trouble. Chickens have been fully domesticated in China since 2000 B.C., apparently having reached there from Burma.

The wild ancestor of the domesticated chicken is a bird called the red jungle fowl, a member of the pheasant family. This bird looks surprisingly like a modern-day red rooster. Many varieties of chicken retain enough of their instincts to raise their own young. However, between the red jungle fowl and today's chickens a surprising change has taken place. Chickens, like many other birds, incubate their eggs by sitting on them. A jungle fowl hen, on the other hand, buries her eggs in the ground, just deep enough to hide them, yet near enough to the surface for the sun to keep them warm until they are ready to hatch. Scientists do not know just when in their evolution chickens modified this very important behavior pattern.

On small farms where chickens are still allowed to range freely, they clearly exhibit their natural, rigidly stratified society, which is organized in the so-called peck order. Each hen has her own place in this order; at the top is the hen who can peck any other in the flock. Just below her is one that can peck any but the top hen. Below her is another who can peck all hens but the top two, and so on, to the bottom, where there is one poor hen who can peck no other, but who may be pecked by all the hens in the flock. Once the order has been established, it does not take a great deal of disciplinary pecking to maintain it, although some of the hens near the bottom of the order take on a rather shabby appearance from too much pecking. The peck order determines which hens get priority at feeding time, which get the choice roosting places, and so on. The cocks have their own separate peck order. Usually the one at the top is the one who does most of the breeding.

Some modern hens retain enough of their instinctive behavior to successfully incubate and hatch a batch of chicks, but in many breeds these instincts have been bred out.

Through the ages chickens have served man well because they are excellent scavengers. In many parts of the world no one would think of feeding a chicken—their job is to make their own living. They eat all kinds of waste materials, picking through manure for the odd undigested kernel of corn, eating bugs, greens, garbage, maggots, turning it all into fine meat and eggs. Farmers have long known that the waste from one pig will support a couple of hens. Chickens are also extremely efficient converters of feed into meat. They require far less feed per pound of added body weight than does a steer or a pig.

Despite the self-sufficient nature of chickens, free range does have its drawbacks. Most hens are artists at hiding their eggs. If their owner is detective enough to find a nest and begin taking the eggs for himself, the hen will probably choose a

new, more secret spot, and the game of hide-and-seek continues. In order to have every egg available for human consumption, chicken farmers have moved their birds inside, and may keep tens of thousands under one roof, in a building that is virtually an egg factory. Starting with breeds of chicken that have lost their desire to incubate their own eggs, egg farmers put three birds in one cage, feed and water them, carry their manure away, and collect their eggs with automatic equipment. Because chickens tend to shed their feathers, or moult, and stop laying temporarily when the days get shorter, these modern chickens never see a short day. Their production is stimulated by artificial light, which keeps their "days" the proper length for the highest production.

Normally, chickens crowded together in wire cages would mutilate or kill each other

by pecking, since their usual defense—
removing themselves to a safe distance—is
impossible. To prevent this, caged chickens
have the points of their beaks burned off as
chicks.

At the end of about a year of such forced
production, commercial egg-producing hens
are spent, and are sold off for meat, to be
replaced by young pullets. Under the less
intense conditions of a small, free-ranging
flock, a hen can keep laying for several
years, although her first year is usually her
most productive, and she does take a rest
every winter to moult.

*Heads down and hackles up,
two cocks face off for a battle.
Game cocks like these two are
still raised for the cruel sport of
cock fighting, although it is il-
legal in this country. When
sharp spurs are tied to the
cocks' own natural spurs, they
often cut each other to ribbons
and both combatants may end
up dead.*

105

A bumblebee, larger and more furry than a honey bee, feeds on nectar and pollen just like its small relative.

The Bumblebee

Bumblebees are close relatives of honey bees. Both belong to the family Apidae (thus the derivation of the word *apiary*), and they live in similar ways. While most other species of bee live solitary lives, both honey bees and bumblebees live in communities. Most bumblebee species nest underground. Usually they make use of a rodent's abandoned burrow, but sometimes they settle in a bird's nest or the space beneath the eaves of a house.

Only queen bees live through the winter. In spring each solitary queen starts building a nest from bits of plants. After warming the nest with her body for a few days she starts to secrete wax from her abdomen. She builds some cells, filling one extra-large cell with honey, to serve as a food source in bad weather and at night. Then she places balls of pollen in another cell, and lays 8 to 12 eggs in with it. She sits on the eggs like a mother hen, keeping them warm and feeding the larvae as they develop. These first eggs hatch into small workers, which then take over all the duties of the hive so that the queen is free to spend her time laying eggs.

Toward the end of summer a group of males and fertile females hatch out, and these bees fly off and mate. The males soon die, but the new queens seek out places to hibernate until spring. Although they never build up the immense colonies that honey bees do, bumblebee hives can number in the thousands. Bumblebees have abilities that honey bees lack. They have extremely long tongues, which allow them to collect nectar from such flowers as red clover and snapdragons, which other insects cannot penetrate. Bumblebees can also start feeding earlier in the morning than other bees. All bees have to warm up their flying muscles before they can take off. The large size and insulating fur of the bumblebee keep it warm so it can make several foraging trips on cool mornings, with no competition from colder-blooded types.

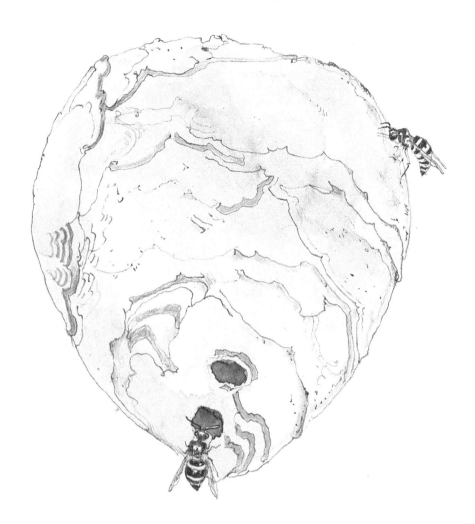

A hornets' nest sometimes takes on strange bands of color when the insects have used splinters of painted wood to build it.

The Wasp

Wasps are among the many insects that seem to have been put on earth to plague us. Like bees, they sting, a notable drawback from our point of view. However, there are many mild-mannered species of wasp that sting only when they are disturbed. There are other, gnat-sized wasps that live as parasites of such pests as alfalfa weevils and houseflies, and do not sting us at all.

The large "paper" wasp nests that can be seen hanging from tree branches and the eaves of houses and barns are built by largish wasps called hornets. Inside the nests, these wasps build a series of horizontal combs, each enclosed by the same "papier-mâché" that covers the outside. To make

this material the hornets collect rotten wood and plant stems, then chew them into a paste which they moisten with saliva. When this material dries it turns into the familiar papery material. These nests are very well insulated, because for every comb that is added inside, a fresh coating is applied to the outside.

Many wasps, including the common yellowjacket, feed on sweet food. For this reason they often turn up as unwanted guests at picnics, hoping to share the jelly from a sandwich or sample a ripe piece of fruit. Orchards are often full of yellow-jackets feeding on fallen, overripe fruit. Like hornets, yellowjackets build paper nests, but theirs are underground. Yellowjackets are fierce defenders of their territory, and may painfully disrupt the country ramble of an innocent walker.

The queen feeds her first batch of larvae herself but, as in honey bee hives, the workers take over the work as soon as they mature. Wasp colonies do not winter over, but produce queens and males that fly out and mate. Once this happens the heart seems to go out of the colony. The insects fail to care for the last batch of larvae, and the old queen lays no more eggs. Gradually the colony dies out.

Two hornets feed on a sweet, late summer pear.

109

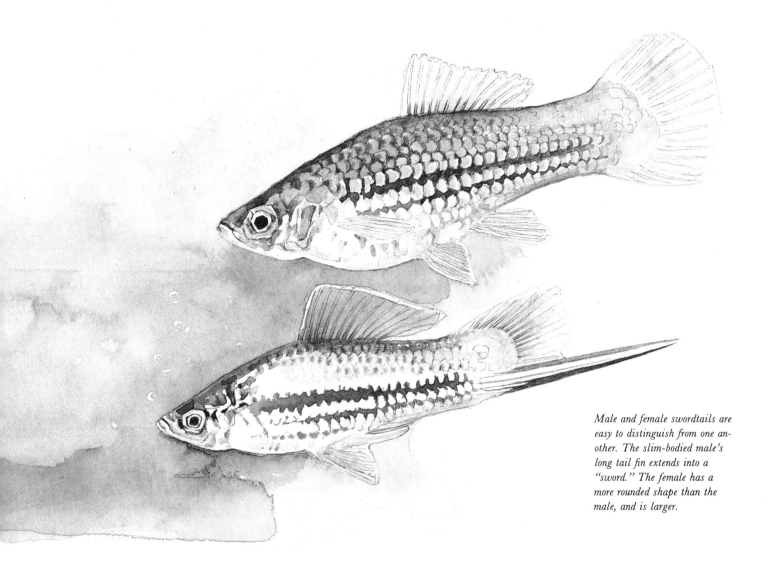

*Male and female swordtails are
easy to distinguish from one another. The slim-bodied male's
long tail fin extends into a
"sword." The female has a
more rounded shape than the
male, and is larger.*

The Platy
and the Swordtail

Two of the most perenially popular home
aquarium fish are the platys and the swordtails. They belong to a family of fish known
as topminnows, because they rise to the surface of the water to feed. Both of these fish
give birth to fully formed babies, rather
than laying eggs like most other kinds of
fish. The males have highly modified anal
fins called gonopodia, which they use to fertilize the female's eggs internally. Other
members of this family include the familiar
guppy, perhaps the most common of all
tropical fish. Another family member is an

aggressive little fish called gambusia, which
devours mosquito larvae with such voracity
that it has been exported from its home in
the southeastern United States to many
parts of the world to help control mosquito
populations.

Live-bearers, as aquarium keepers usually
call swordtails, platys and their relatives,
bear hundreds of young at a time, then
quickly gobble them up, unless their tank
has been planted heavily with fine grasses
for the babies to hide in. Males will often
follow females, just waiting for the babies to

emerge so they can eat them. However, this bizarre and counterproductive behavior has not been observed in the fish's natural habitat in Central America. Probably it is caused by the crowded conditions of a small tank, which force the fish closer than they would naturally choose to be.

Swordtails and platys have received a great deal of attention from the medical profession because they develop a kind of cancer that appears to be genetically determined. When a green swordtail is crossed with a spotted platy, the resulting young develop cancers on the sides of their bodies. These tumors are quite similar to some kinds of human cancers, a fact that has caused some investigators to speculate that the human tumors may also have a genetic origin. Interestingly, although the two fish that have these diseased offspring can be bred in captivity, and although the two species live side by side in streams in Mexico and Central America, they do not interbreed in the wild.

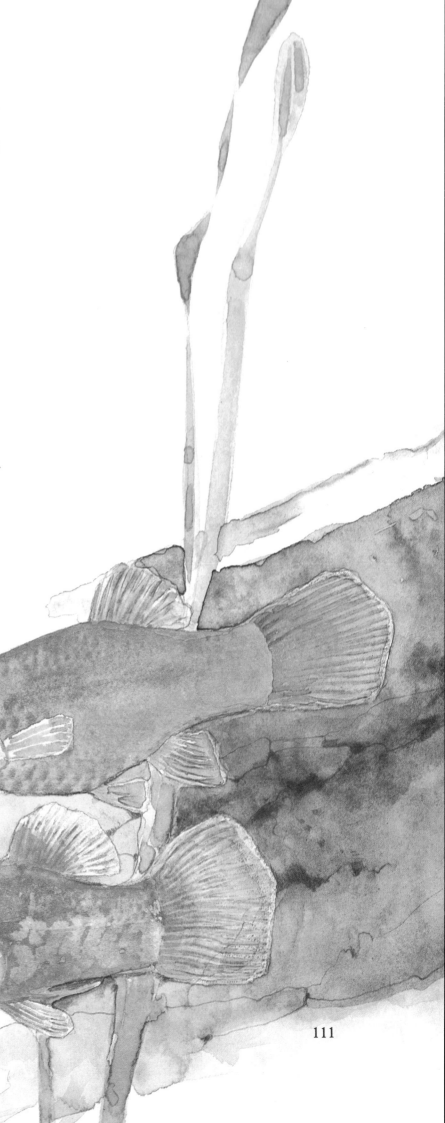

Aquarium keepers have bred platys in a vast range of colors, from the gold of these two to dark and shimmering greens. Platys and swordtails are exceptionally easy to breed and raise in home aquariums.

111

A farm cat prowls through a meadow on the lookout for an unwary mouse or bird. Country cats can be self-sufficient predators, at least in warm weather, although they welcome a warm stove-side cushion or a pan of fresh milk in the barn.

The Cat

Rudyard Kipling called him "the cat that walked by himself." Though cats have been domesticated for thousands of years, they have never accepted the yoke of servitude as other domestic animals have. They are domestic only by consent; they preserve the right not only to slip back into the wild at any time but also to return to the easy food and warm comfort of home when they please. It used to be said that "a cat can look at a king," and it is still true. If a person stares at a cat the cat will stare back, and it is usually the person who blinks and looks away first.

Most people either love cats or hate them. There seems to be little neutral ground. A recent study showed that business executives, who presumably enjoy power and control more than most people, fall generally into the category of cat haters. Artists, on the other hand, seem to have a type of personality that takes pleasure in the cat's independent nature.

Over the ages human attitudes toward cats have fluctuated widely. The ancient Egyptians worshipped cats, possibly because they destroyed the rats and mice that wreaked havoc in their granaries. When a

Cats spend much of their time
in quiet activities like washing
and sleeping. Because they have
a proportionately small amount
of blood, compared to active animals like dogs, they must conserve their metabolic energy.
However, they can move like
lightning in short bursts, catching a mouse, or spitting and
hissing to defend themselves
from a dog.

Kittens practice adult skills by playing, just as children do. Here they develop muscles and reflexes they will need for hunting and fighting.

An angry kitten dances sideways with his tail puffed out like a bottle brush. A cat's expression changes as the animal grows suspicious and then angry. Its ears flatten and move back; its whiskers draw back and its pupils dilate.

pet cat died, its owner shaved off his eyebrows in mourning. The cat might be mummified and buried in a special cat cemetery. Statues of ancient Egyptian cats, which we can still see in museums, look strikingly similar to the regal Siamese cat.

In contrast to the reverent treatment they received from Egyptians, cats suffered horrible cruelties during the Middle Ages, when they were feared and hated as witches' associates. In this country some people still believe that it is unlucky to have a black cat cross their path, while in Great Britain it is taken as a good omen.

Much of the behavior of a domestic cat differs little from that of its wild relatives, such as the lion or ocelot. Even a house cat covers its feces, as if to escape detection by a predator. Cats hunt by stealth like their wild relatives. They creep up on a mouse or a bird on silent feet, until they are close

114

enough for the final pounce. Cats often seem to torture their prey by playing with it for a long time without killing it. This behavior has little to do with whether or not the cat is hungry. It happens because the cat must build up a high level of excitement before it is stimulated to dispatch its prey. This excitement comes from catching and re-catching the victim.

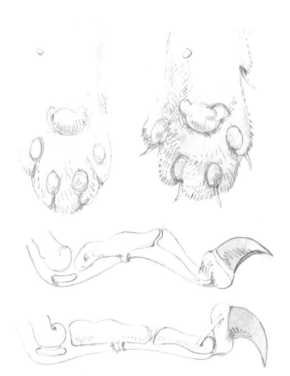

Cats can extend and withdraw their claws using two muscles—a short band near the claw, which contracts to pull it in, and another attached to a long tendon, which pulls the claw out when it is tightened.

A cat's eyes seem to glow in the dark because its retinas have a shiny layer that reflect the light that reaches it. Thus light passes the retina's receptor cells twice, intensifying dim images, and allowing cats to see in almost complete darkness.

115

The Swan

Two mute swans float affectionately together. Swans generally mate for life. Below, a male raises his wings and arches his neck to threaten an opponent.

The mute swan, which originally lived only in Europe and Asia, was introduced into this country in the middle of the nineteenth century, probably first on some of the large estates on Long Island and along the Hudson River. These elegant creatures, quite common now, may be seen in amusement parks and zoos, and some have taken up life in the wild. In fact, along parts of the East Coast, on Michigan lakes and in Washington's Puget Sound, where sizeable populations have built up, they have become pests.

116

Wild mute swans can fly fifty to fifty-five miles per hour. However, park swans generally have their wings clipped to prevent them from flying off with their wild brethren.

The males are extremely aggressive, and one male will take over an entire pond or small lake for the use of himself and his mate and cygnets. He will chase out any intruder, and can seriously injure a small child.

In England mute swans are called royal swans because they have long been controlled by the Crown, which granted certain nobles and corporations the right to keep them. Perhaps because of their association with the royal family, these swans have more pubs named after them than any other bird or animal.

Throughout history swans have been venerated, maybe because their pristine white feathers suggest purity. Swans have served as the emblem of the Virgin Mary, and in many legends princes and knights appear as swans. Swans are both fierce fighters and faithful mates, so they fit right in with the ideals of chivalry.

Swans are also solicitous parents. A day after the cygnets hatch they can swim, but they never go out onto the water without the protection of their parents. The female, or "pen," swims ahead of her babies while the father, or "cob," follows, guarding them from an attack from the rear.

In addition to the mute swan, the United States is host to two native species. The trumpeter is so called for its loud rasping call. This swan looks almost exactly like the mute, except for a black bill with a yellow stripe at the base called the "grin line." During the nineteenth century the trumpeter was hunted almost to extinction, but government intervention and a successful conservation program has now restored its numbers to a level high enough to ensure its survival as a species. The other native species is the whistling swan, which has a higher-pitched call than the trumpeter, although it is not a true whistle. This bird has been heard to sing a true "swan song" as it falls dying after having been shot.

Domestic geese threaten in-truders by pointing their heads up and hissing. Geese make ef-fective watchdogs; they are quite aggressive and may kill small dogs and injure children.

The Goose

Geese, like dogs, have been domesticated for a very long time. All of the modern breeds except the Chinese are descended from the wild European graylag goose. In China, geese have been domesticated for around three thousand years; some historians believe that the process of domesticating the graylag began in Europe in the late Stone Age, tens of thousands of years ago.

Besides providing the tastiest of Christmas dinners, geese have long served mankind by providing the feathers used to make quills. Before the large-scale production of metal pen tips in the nineteenth century, people wrote mainly with goose feathers. The hollow stem had just the right diameter to hold the ink, and the right flexibility for forming letters. The soft inner feathers are still valued. Collectively they are called "down," and, for winter clothing, they are the best-known insulation. Although down is expensive compared to various synthetic insulations, many mountain climbers, skiers and snowmobilers insist on down for their cold-weather gear.

Besides being useful, geese are exceptionally interesting animals to have around. A little study reveals that they communicate largely by posture. The male can be identified by the upright set of his head and neck, while the female bends her head a little in submission. When a baby goose hatches, it attaches itself, emotionally, to the first object it sees, through a process called imprinting. Goslings hatched in an incubator will imprint on whomever they first see. Whether that first creature is goose or human, the gosling will accept it as "mother" for the rest of its life. In the wild, of course, this process works well because the first object a gosling sees is most likely to be its own mother. But under domestic conditions, imprinting can lead to some strange situations. Konrad Lorenz, the famed Austrian animal behaviorist, tells the story of a goose he owned that was raised with a flock of chickens. When the goose matured, Lorenz went out and found her a gander, expecting the pair would mate and raise goslings. But she had long ago imprinted on a chicken, and so loved only the rooster. She paid no attention to the gander, but harassed the rooster constantly, jealously keeping him from his flock, and making his life thoroughly miserable.

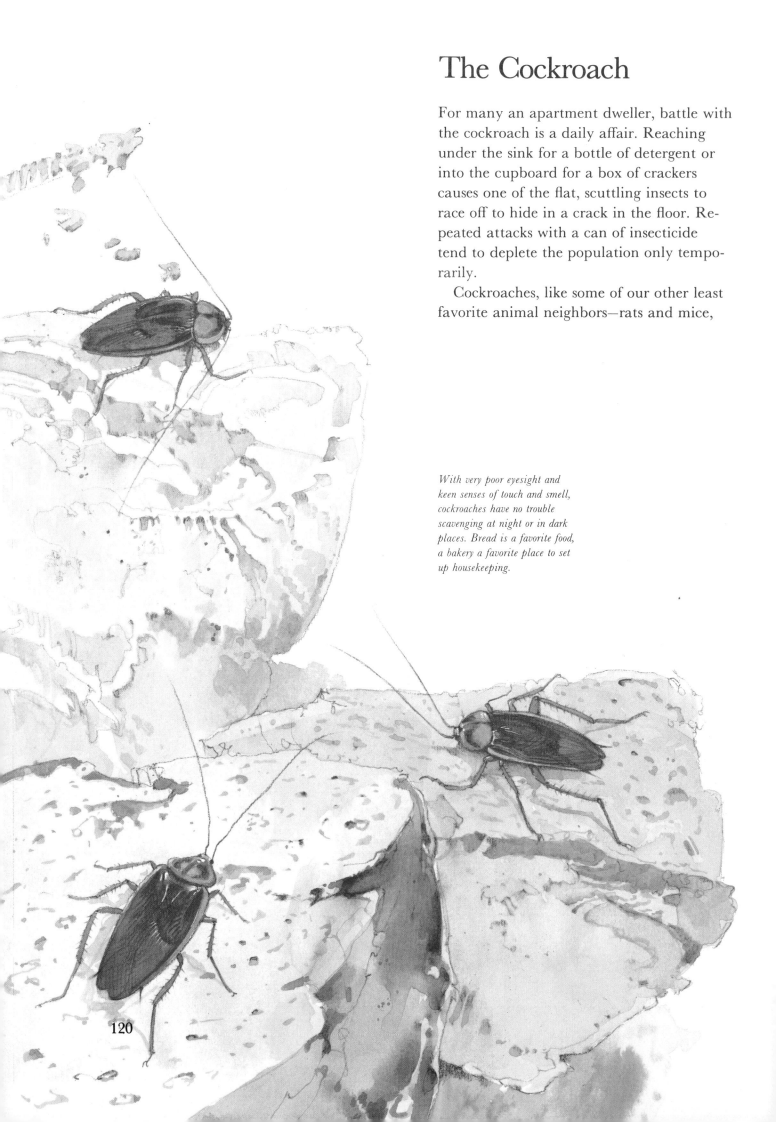

The Cockroach

For many an apartment dweller, battle with the cockroach is a daily affair. Reaching under the sink for a bottle of detergent or into the cupboard for a box of crackers causes one of the flat, scuttling insects to race off to hide in a crack in the floor. Repeated attacks with a can of insecticide tend to deplete the population only temporarily.

Cockroaches, like some of our other least favorite animal neighbors—rats and mice,

With very poor eyesight and keen senses of touch and smell, cockroaches have no trouble scavenging at night or in dark places. Bread is a favorite food, a bakery a favorite place to set up housekeeping.

120

for instance—have made a way of life for themselves based on man's food, garbage and warmth. One researcher who made a study of the contents of cockroach stomachs described their diet as consisting of "boiled potatoes, vegetables, cereal, dough, dead and diseased cockroaches, chocolate, honey, butter, vaseline, bread flour, sugar, leather, wool, cloth fibers, shoe polish and book bindings."

In general, cockroaches congregate where there is warmth and a plentiful supply of sweet or starchy food. For this reason they have been a plague in bakeries and restaurants throughout history. With the advent of modern insecticides, cockroaches have become easier to control. But new strains are developing that are resistant to almost every known insecticide. It is likely that cockroaches will be among us for some time to come. They are among the world's oldest insects, and they are so adaptable to changing conditions that their shape and body organization have changed very little for the last 230 million years. Insects very similar to the ones we see today were some of the very first animals to inhabit the earth.

Most species of cockroach do not invade human dwellings, and most live in tropical regions because they require more warmth than is available in temperate zones. They die if the temperature falls below 20° F, but can survive up to 120°. Most of the outdoor species feed on decaying vegetation. Few of them can fly well, but rely on running fast to escape their predators.

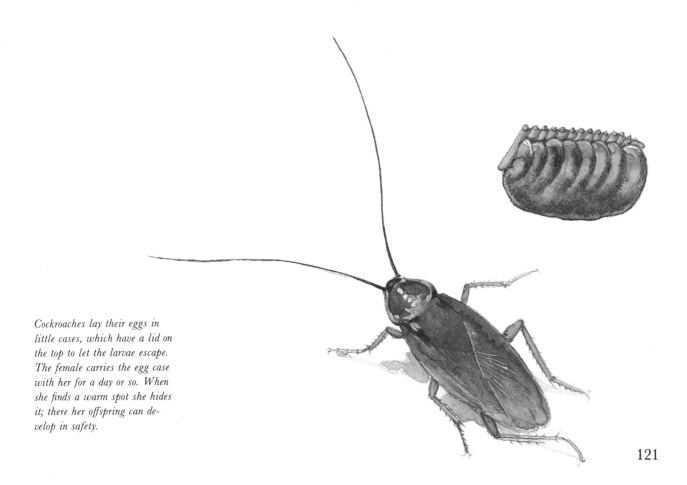

Cockroaches lay their eggs in little cases, which have a lid on the top to let the larvae escape. The female carries the egg case with her for a day or so. When she finds a warm spot she hides it; there her offspring can develop in safety.

The all-white Saanen is one of the breeds of domestic goat that has been developed specifically for milk production.

The Goat

Dairy farmers, accustomed to their highly productive Holstein cows, tend to refer to goats condescendingly as "the poor man's cow." However, dairy goats are really more efficient milk producers than most cows. In proportion to her body weight, a good goat gives more milk than a cow, and she does it on less feed. In addition, she has a much more efficient rate of reproduction, bearing 2 or more kids a year, on the average, while a cow usually has only 1 calf.

Goats are not likely to usurp the dairy cow's position as the world's main milk supplier, however. To get the milk that one cow can give, a farmer would have to milk eight or nine goats. In a society in which labor is expensive, the goat's greater efficiency cannot make up for the increased labor costs.

Goats were first domesticated in western Asia about ten thousand years ago from Persian wild goats that roamed the land in large herds. When explorers first began to cross oceans and discover new lands, they

took goats with them to provide fresh meat and milk. Some of these animals escaped or were traded away at ports along the way, and so they spread throughout the world. When goats were dropped off on islands with no natural predators, their populations often rose to such high levels that they stripped off all the vegetation, and chopped up the soil with their sharp hooves, turning what had once been lush forests and meadows into virtual deserts. Goats, being descended from mountain-climbing ancestors, are agile enough to kill trees by climbing up into them and stripping off their leaves.

Although goats do eat a great variety of plant material, they are not the tin can and clothes eaters of legend. They may pull clothes off the line because they are curious animals who seem to want a hand in whatever is going on around them. Except for a dog, a goat probably makes as playful and affectionate a pet as any animal. Goats are extremely social, and if one is kept alone it will bleat plaintively most of the time out

Goats love to climb, and will take advantage of a rock or a platform like this one to jump up and play "king of the mountain."

Two goat kids (below), a white Saanen and a brown Toggenburg, face off, rearing and butting heads in a mock contest. Such behavior was useful to wild goats, as it prepared them to fight for mates as adults.

of sheer loneliness. Goats are also amazingly deft at getting out of enclosures, so anyone who is planning to keep a goat must be prepared to build a strong, high fence, and even then spend a certain amount of time rounding up his pet and putting it back in its pen.

123

The Swallow
and the Swift

Some of our familiar birds, such as robins and doves, are most often seen when they are on the ground, feeding. But others, like the swallows and swifts, are almost always seen in the air. These birds, in fact, spend most of their time flying, collecting insects in their gaping mouths. All of them have weak legs that are not well adapted for walking. Martins do spend some time on the ground, but swifts have such weak legs that they can barely get up in the air again if they happen to land on the ground.

The purple martin, which is a member of the swallow family, is a bird most eagerly cultivated by bird lovers. It has a great reputation as a mosquito eater, although it eats many kinds of insects, including ants, grasshoppers, wasps, dragonflies, caterpillars and moths. Martins can be seen flying low over the surface of the water. Often the birds will take a sip of water as they fly, or even dip the back ends of their bodies into the water for a bath.

Purple martins are something of a puzzle because they do not live in many of the places that seem to be entirely suitable for them. It is a triumph to build a martin

124

A purple martin house is usually built with many rooms, as the birds like to nest in colonies. One large house built by a man in New Jersey held two hundred seventy pairs of birds.

house and actually get a colony of martins living in it. Building martin houses is an old custom, one that started with the Indians, who used to hang up gourds for the birds to nest in.

Barn swallows, like martins, have little fear of man, and live in close association with us. Most barns in the country have barn swallow nests under the eaves or on the rafters. At dusk and dawn during nesting season the air is full of forked-tailed swallows swooping in and out of barns, carrying insects back to their babies in the nest. When the babies grow big enough to

climb out of their nest, but are not yet able to fly, the parent birds seem to become almost hysterically nervous, swooping down over the head of any dog, cat or person who comes near the nest, in an effort to drive them away.

Swallows are migratory birds, and they return faithfully to the same nests every spring. Legend has it that the cliff swallows return every year on March 19 to the San Juan Capistrano Mission in southern California. However, the swallows are not perfect in their accuracy; they go north with warm weather, like other migrants, and

Baby barn swallows perch on the edge of their nest begging for food. To keep them satisfied, their parents have to feed them three hundred times a day.

vary their arrival time by a few days from year to year.

Swifts look like swallows but are not related to them. Their similar lifestyle has caused them to evolve in similar ways. Swallows usually have forked tails, and swifts have blunt ones, but there are some exceptions to this rule. Swallows usually fly more erratically, and closer to the ground, than do the high-flying swifts.

Swifts spend most of their time on the wing. One ornithologist banded a swift that lived for 9 years. He kept track of its movements and estimated that it flew 1,350,000 miles during its lifetime, includ-

ing its yearly migration to South America and back.

Some European swifts even spend their nights flying. Chimney swifts, however, roost at night, and, as their name suggests, like to settle down in chimneys. At dusk they enter a chimney and cling to its inner walls, hanging on with their sharp claws and propping themselves up with strong bristled tails. One observer in Pennsylvania watched ten thousand swifts enter a huge factory chimney in thirty-seven minutes. Inside, the birds rested in overlapping rows.

Chimney swifts build their nests with twigs that they break off in flight. They glue these together with sticky saliva. Because they usually build their nests in chimneys, many young swifts are killed when a late spring cold snap causes people to light a fire in the stove or turn on the furnace, blasting hot air up the chimney.

126

Chimney swifts circle a chimney for an hour at sunset before
gradually settling down to roost
inside it for the night.

127

An adult longhorn beetle crawls
over the timbers of an old house.
Inside, its larvae bore through
the soft wood, making tunnels
that weaken the beams.

The Longhorn Beetle

In the days when woodstoves were the main source of heat, householders were on more familiar terms with the longhorn beetle than are the homeowners of today. It was no surprise to hear one of the logs stacked next to the fireplace clicking, or making a sawing noise. During a warm spell, when the log might sit waiting its turn for a day or so, a pile of sawdust would grow beneath it. These ghostly manifestations were actually the work of the larvae of one of the twelve hundred North American species of longhorn beetle.

Most longhorn species are long-bodied, in contrast to the round-bodied beetles, such as the ladybug and Japanese beetle. Most of them also have extremely long antennae, often up to three times longer than their bodies. Many species, like the wasp beetle, are beautifully colored, and are eagerly sought by insect collectors. In most species, the adults eat such plant materials as wood, leaves and pollen. Some of the brightly colored species feed on flowers. It is the larvae of the beetles, rather than the adults, who come into the house with the firewood, however. At this stage of their lives, the young insects are white, and are called round-headed borers. They make tunnels in the wood, and can do a great deal of damage in the lumber industry by digging through cut logs. Usually the adult beetles lay their eggs in trees, beneath the bark. When the eggs hatch, the larvae dig their way further inside. In some species the larvae live for a long time before pupating and maturing. One species often found in the wood of old houses spends 12 to 15 years in the larval stage, and one individual larva was known to live for 32 years before becoming an adult.

Although longhorn beetles damage forests and lumber, people no longer fear them; in the past, these chewing beetles were widely regarded as harbingers of death and called "death watch beetles."

Protective coloration enables the wasp beetle to escape many predators. So closely does it resemble a wasp that many birds who enjoy the taste of beetles, but fear wasps, are afraid to touch it.

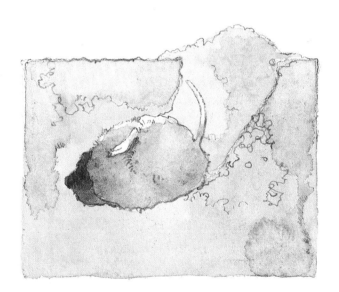

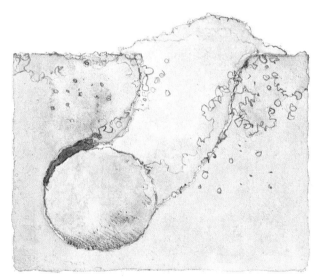

Black and red sexton beetles
bury a dead shrew by digging a
slanting tunnel under it so that
it falls into the ground. They
help it down by shoving it and
rolling it into a ball. Some beetles have buried small mammals
and birds two feet deep, though
most of their graves are only a
few inches below the surface.

The Sexton Beetle

The sexton beetle is named after church sextons, whose job it once was to dig graves for their parishioners. Although most modern sextons no longer bury the dead, their beetle namesakes are still at it.

Sexton beetles locate dead animals and birds by their odor. When a male discovers a carcass, he signals for a mate by calling with a raucous cry, and by emitting a special scent. The cry also attracts other males, who come and fight with the finder and each other for the prize discovery. When a female arrives, she and the winning male begin to bury their dead animal, as shown in the sequence above. They dig a hollow under the corpse. When it falls in, the beetles cover it with earth. If the ground is too hard for digging, they will drag it to a softer spot.

Once the carcass is buried the beetles are ready to use it for their purposes. The female lays her eggs and then begins to eat the dead animal. The eggs hatch into larvae in 5 days. For the first few days of their life, the babies eat food regurgitated by their parents. The larvae sit in front of their parents like baby birds, with their mouths open waiting for a meal. If one should get pushed aside, a parent will pick it up with its front legs and feed it. After 4 or 5 days the young are able to feed directly from the carcass. Interestingly, adult sexton beetles eat carrion only when they have young to feed. The rest of the time they eat the insects that are inevitably attracted to dead animals.

131

Two male eastern fence lizards threaten each other by displaying their colorful blue throat patches.

The Lizard

Lizards, although they are a common sight, seem to evoke the distant past. A fence lizard sunning itself, or even a pet chameleon flicking its long tongue out at a fly, could have walked right out of the age of dinosaurs into the twentieth century. They are smaller than their ancient cousins, but their shape and manner have changed little.

Though their heritage is ancient, lizards are well adapted to conditions in the modern world. Because they are not highly intelligent animals they have had to evolve some rather strange ways of doing things. Many lizards, for instance, can hardly recognize the sex of another member of their own species. In order for a male to find out

whether another lizard is a prospective mate, or an opponent, he makes threatening gestures: some flash their colored bellies; others adopt specific postures or gaits. If the threatened lizard also makes threats, it is recognized as a male. If it does not, it is by default a female, and mating can proceed.

Like all reptiles, lizards are cold-blooded. They cannot regulate their temperatures internally, as mammals can, nor do they have an insulating cover of fur or feathers. They are much more dependent on the temperature of the environment than warm-blooded animals. In warm weather they are quick and active, but they slow down as the temperature drops, and many hibernate. Dur-

132

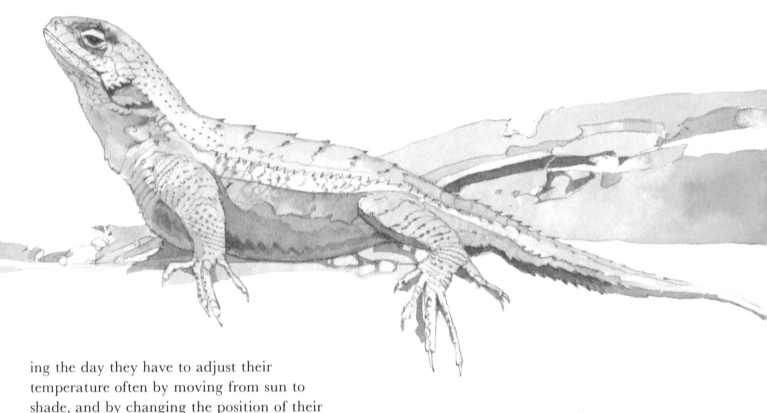

ing the day they have to adjust their temperature often by moving from sun to shade, and by changing the position of their body relative to the direction of the sun's rays.

One of the ways that lizards differ from most other vertebrates is that some of them can reproduce parthenogenically—that is, without fertilization. There are two species that have no males at all, the females producing other females without the intervention of a male. In some other species there are a few males, but a huge preponderance of females, and these species probably reproduce parthenogenically some of the time. What advantage this method of reproduction provides is still a mystery.

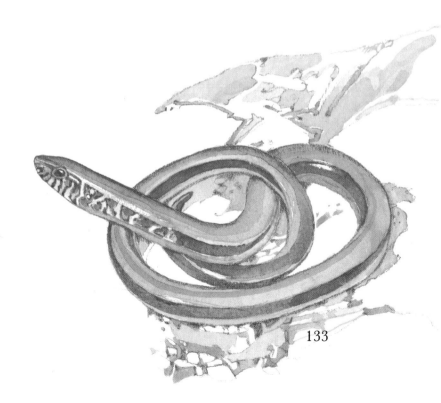

The eastern glass lizard is one of a family of legless lizards. Their bodies are stiff with bony armor in the skin, and the vertebrae of their long tails are extremely brittle. When seized by a predator the tail breaks off, its muscles continuing to twitch, occupying the captor while the "victim" escapes and grows a new tail.

133

The Heron

One of the most rewarding sights to greet an early morning canoeist is that of a great blue heron feeding along the edge of a lake, stepping gently among the weeds as the mist rises off the water. If the paddler is careful, he can glide close to the huge grey bird, and watch as it stands motionless waiting for a fish to move, or a small rodent to scuttle along the shore. But with the slap of a paddle or the click of a camera shutter, the heron will rise out of the water, showing its immense 7-foot wingspan, and sail majestically off to find its meal elsewhere.

The heron family comprises sixty-three species, including the bitterns and egrets, as well as herons. They are all long-legged and long-necked, and most of them live in close association with water. It is possible to distinguish a heron in flight from other large water birds, such as storks and geese, because herons fly with their heads drawn back rather than extended in front of them.

As they wade along mucky lakeshores,

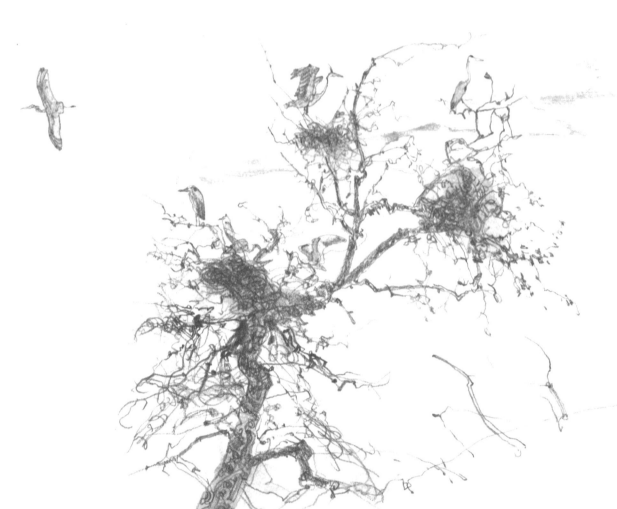

Many herons nest in large groups high in tall trees.

rocky streams or on the beach at seaside, herons feed on frogs, mice, and small fishes and birds. They can stab their prey with their long, sharp bills, which are lethal weapons. One heron stabbed a wooden oar so hard its bill went right through and stuck out two inches on the other side. However, this bird was wounded and frightened; a healthy heron would not allow an oar near it.

The most widely distributed North American heron is the green heron, which is much less spectacular than the great blue heron or the snowy egret. The green heron is about 1½ feet tall, and inhabits almost every stream pond and stream in the southern United States.

Probably our most beautiful heron is the snowy egret. This bird has spotless white plumage, and during the breeding season it grows even more magnificent, sprouting long waving plumes on its head, neck and back. These plumes nearly caused the bird's

extinction toward the end of the nineteenth century, as the egrets were heavily hunted for their plumage. However, the National Audubon Society, along with other conservation organizations, was instrumental in getting protective legislation passed, and the species has now recovered.

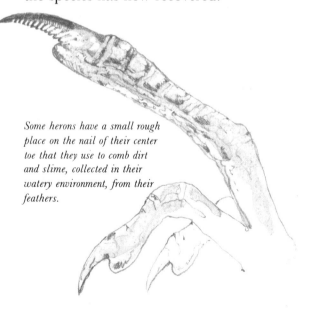

Some herons have a small rough place on the nail of their center toe that they use to comb dirt and slime, collected in their watery environment, from their feathers.

The Rat

There is probably no animal on earth that disgusts people more than the rat. Unfortunately, there is good reason for this feeling. Epidemiologists estimate that diseases spread by rats have killed more people throughout history than all the wars we have ever had. The two species that have caused almost all of the trouble are the black rat and the Norway, or brown, rat. Neither of these was native to the United States—or to any other part of the Western Hemisphere. Both probably originated in Asia. The black rat was the first to spread through Europe, arriving in the Middle Ages. It was carried to the New World on ships that arrived in Central America in the sixteenth century, and it came to this country in 1609 with the Jamestown colonists. Black rats are also known as "ships' rats" because they are especially adept at coming aboard ships and making their way to new ports. They are excellent climbers, and often used to enter ships by running up the lines that tied them to the wharf.

In this country black rats have settled mainly in the South, where they live in the upper stories of buildings and make their nests in trees and vines. Their preferred food is grain, but they will eat almost anything.

The Norway rat is a more aggressive species than the black rat, and has moved in and taken over many areas, pushing the black rats out. The name Norway rat is a misnomer. There are no more Norway rats in Norway than there are anywhere else,

The black rat is one of two species that plague mankind. It is not really black, but is brown to grey on top, with light parts underneath.

A litter of young rats has been known to get their tails tangled in a knot, and all starve to death.

and they did not originate there. They, too, came from Asia, spreading throughout Europe between the sixteenth and eighteenth centuries. They reached America in the late eighteenth century with mercenaries the British hired to fight in the Revolutionary War.

In the country, Norway rats dig ground nests, with various tunnels and chambers. In more built-up areas, they frequently live in sewers or cellars. Like black rats, they will eat anything that people eat. They are fierce hunters, and will kill and eat chickens, as well as chicken eggs. They forage mostly at night, and farmers have learned never to feed their chickens at night, or they will end up feeding rats instead of fowl. Rats have even been known to gnaw into large animals, such as pigs, and have killed elephants in zoos by gnawing holes in their feet, which then become fatally infected.

Brown rats live in large colonies and will fight intruders from other groups. Female rats mate with several males, and carry their litters of about 8 for 24 days. A female can mate again immediately after delivering a litter, and so is theoretically capable

137

Two brown rats from different colonies fight fiercely when one enters the other's territory. Rat bites can cause severe infections, even to other rats.

Albino rats like this mother and litter have been laboratory bred from Norway rats and used extensively in scientific and medical research. For all the harm wild rats have caused humanity, their white cousins may have done an equal amount of good.

of having 12 litters a year. However, 5 is more usual. In a large colony nursing females may care for babies of other mothers as well as their own.

Rats have extremely strong and sharp incisor teeth, which can do a great deal of damage. They can easily chew through walls to get into houses or grain storage bins. They have started fires by chewing through the insulation on wiring, and have even chewed holes in dams and caused floods. Water doesn't bother them because they are excellent swimmers.

Throughout history people have tried to get rid of rats, but the animals just find new ways to survive. Because they like exactly the same kinds of conditions as people, it probably will not be possible to eradicate

them while human beings exist. Poison will clear rats from an area for a while, but then a strain develops that is immune to the poison. Legend has it that the Pied Piper of Hamelin lured all the rats and mice from the village by playing music that was irresistible to them. However, rats will make mass migrations when conditions get too crowded; it is probable that the Pied Piper was just lucky enough to show up when the rats were leaving anyway.

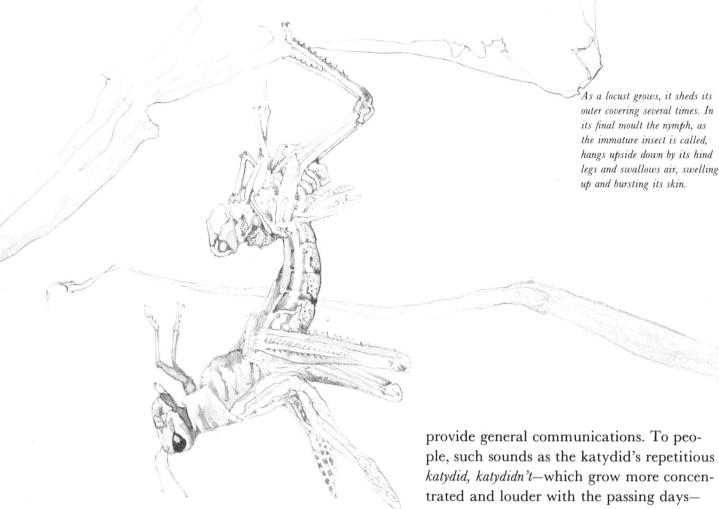

The Grasshopper

Grasshoppers and their relatives, the katydids and the locusts, all belong to the insect order Orthoptera, a name chosen because its members have straight front wings. These insects also have extremely long and strong hind legs, which give them exceptional jumping ability. A grasshopper can jump three feet high—the equivalent of a ninety-foot jump for a man.

On a sunny August day in open country the air is filled with the sounds of grasshopper and katydid calls. Different species make characteristically different sounds, and they make them in different ways. Some species rub a hind leg against a thickened wing vein, causing the wing to vibrate like the string of a violin. Others rub their legs against a rough spot on their bodies, or rub their wings together. The sounds are received by eardrum-like places on the insects' abdomens or legs, and convey different messages. Some are expressions of territorial rights, others attract mates or provide general communications. To people, such sounds as the katydid's repetitious *katydid, katydidn't*—which grow more concentrated and louder with the passing days—signify the coming end of summer.

Grasshoppers do a certain amount of damage to crops by cutting into grasses to lay their eggs, and also by eating vegetation. Some species of locust, however, can do terrible damage. At times they will mass together and go into a frenzy of breeding. They build a population numbering in the billions, then migrate. When they do, they devastate the areas they pass through, stripping off all vegetation, and even eating wood. Plagues of locusts that caused terrible famines are described in the Bible, and one almost destroyed the first Mormon settlement in Utah. The settlers were dramatically spared when a flock of California gulls showed up and consumed the insects. Locust plagues still occur, mostly in Africa, South America and the Middle East. Migrations tend to follow the same paths, and some areas are repeatedly devastated.

For a long time it was thought that migratory and non-migratory locusts belonged to separate species. The two do look different, but entomologists have discovered that the difference is purely chemical. When they prepare to migrate, locusts

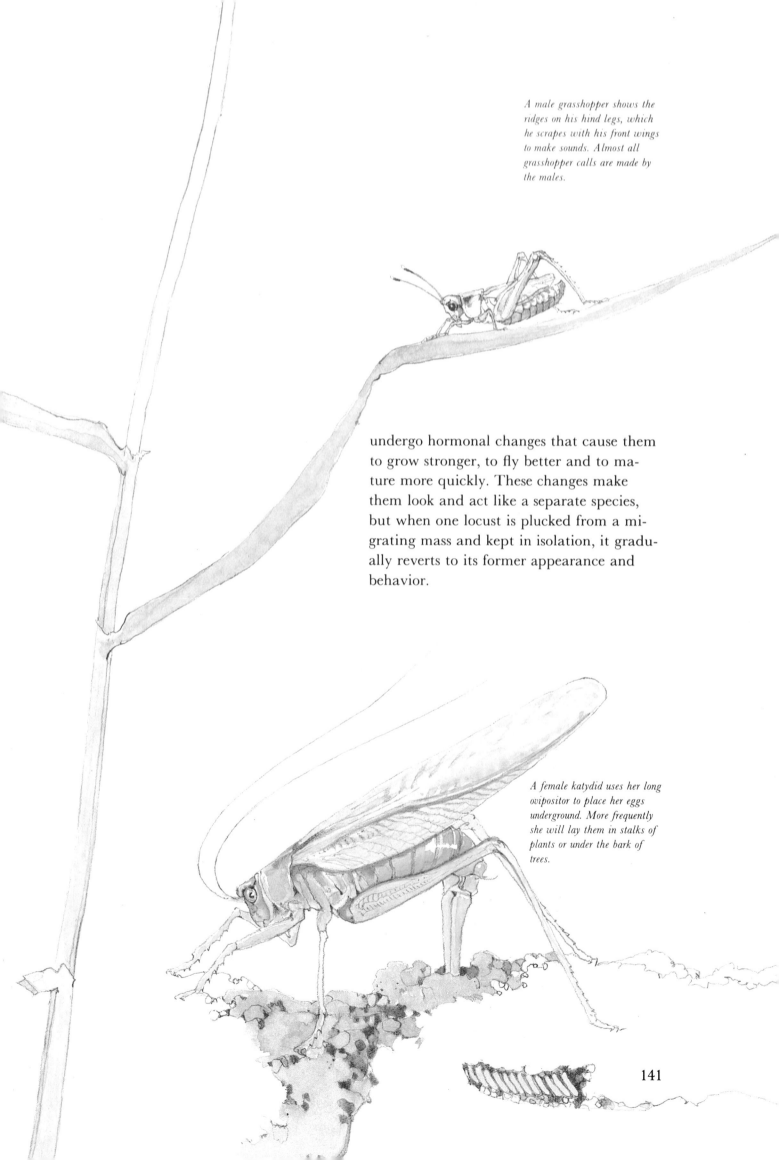

A male grasshopper shows the ridges on his hind legs, which he scrapes with his front wings to make sounds. Almost all grasshopper calls are made by the males.

undergo hormonal changes that cause them to grow stronger, to fly better and to mature more quickly. These changes make them look and act like a separate species, but when one locust is plucked from a migrating mass and kept in isolation, it gradually reverts to its former appearance and behavior.

A female katydid uses her long ovipositor to place her eggs underground. More frequently she will lay them in stalks of plants or under the bark of trees.

The Cricket

A cricket is one of the few insects that most people welcome into their houses. Although it can be a nuisance to have a house cricket chirping through the night, most people regard it as a sign of good luck, or at least as an acceptable visitor.

In the fall two kinds of cricket may appear in the house. One is the brown cricket, which lives indoors all year round. It lives on scraps of food and lays its eggs throughout the year. It likes warmth, so it is usually

House crickets are brown and slender, with longer legs and antennae than field crickets (top). At left, a male field cricket sits outside his burrow and chirps to attract a mate.

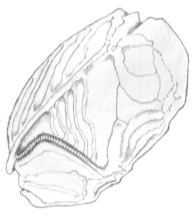

A male cricket makes his chirping sounds by rubbing his wings together. The left wing has a thickened ridge, which the cricket rubs with the file-like edge of his right wing to set up the vibrations.

found in the kitchen near the stove or beside a fireplace. The other is the field cricket, which though it lives mostly outdoors, eating seeds and young plants, as well as dead insects, cannot survive frost. It seeks the warmth of a house as winter approaches. Its eggs are able to survive the winter outside only because the female puts them deep into the soil with a long ovipositor.

Male crickets, like their close relatives the grasshoppers, make sounds to attract their mates. The field cricket rubs its wings together at a rate of 7 times a second. This rapid rubbing produces a tone at 4,200 cycles per second, equivalent to a high C. Its common song is a triple chirp, while its courtship song is a continuous trill.

Male crickets fight fiercely to defend the territories around their burrows. Unfortu-

nately people have found a way to exploit this behavior by holding cricket fights so that they can bet on the outcome. Although crickets will rarely even injure each other in a territorial fight, they will often kill under the artificial conditions imposed by man. In a staged fight the stronger cricket will defeat the weaker, but in nature it is nearly always the cricket closest to its own burrow that wins the fight. To prove this, entomologists took two crickets that had been living in separate containers and let them meet on neutral ground. The two fought repeatedly, and the same one won every time. But when both crickets were put in the weaker one's container, he won every time. His courage and resolve were apparently boosted by being on home ground, while the strong one did not feel so confident there.

When a foal is born, the leg bones from the knee to the foot are as long as they are in a mature horse. These long legs allow wild foals to gallop fast and keep up with the herd when they are only a few hours old.

Two mustang stallions (opposite page) fight for dominance as wild stallions have always done. The victor will be permitted to keep all the mares in the band, while the loser will have to go elsewhere, starting fights until he can find an old stallion he can defeat.

144

The Horse

No animal has had more to do with the development of human civilization than the horse. It has borne men in all but the most recent wars, it has plowed his fields, carried his goods (and his mail) from one culture to another, dragged his produce to market, his doctors to the sick, and his dead to the grave. Who can imagine what deserts might never have been crossed, what civilizations left uninvaded and what prairies left unplowed were it not for the horse? Could the knights have walked to the Crusades? Would soldiers have dragged cannons into battle on foot?

The first use mankind probably found for horses was as a source of meat. There are many prehistoric cave paintings showing men hunting horses. It is not known when horses were first used for riding, but the earliest Hindu legends from India mention horses being sacrificed and used in wars. Some historians speculate that horses were first ridden by men herding cattle.

The horses of today are descended from the species *Equus caballus fossilis,* which roamed the plains of Europe fifty thousand years ago. These little horses were very similar to the only truly wild horse of today, which is called Przewalski's horse. These horses are the size of ponies, yellowish with black manes and tails, and look very much like many of the horses shown in cave paintings.

Modern horses have been bred from two

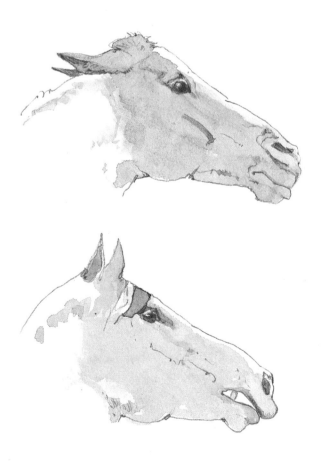

Horses indicate their intent by the position of their ears. An angry horse about to bite or kick first warns by flattening its ears back. An interested, calm horse pricks its ears forward. On the opposite page a stallion, full of energy and good spirits, prances along with his ears forward, while a tired, irritated mare plods along, ears back.

Ponies resemble the ancestral wild horse more than do most of the larger breeds. The Norwegian duns above are the size, shape and color of many of the horses in prehistoric cave paintings. The fat Shetland pony at right is only three feet high and a popular mount for small children.

main strains that lived in Asia and Europe. One was a large, placid animal that lived in forests and on grassy plains. From these horses came the immensely strong "greathorses" that carried the knights in armor, and later our many breeds of draft horses. The other strain of horse was light-boned, fast and high-spirited. This horse was developed into the hot-blooded breeds, such as the Arabian and the thoroughbred race horse of today. Many other breeds have been created by mixing the two original strains to get offspring with varying degrees of strength, speed, calmness or fiery disposition.

Horses were not found in the Western Hemisphere before the coming of the white man. The first ones arrived with Columbus on his second voyage, in 1493. Soon the Spanish conquistadors were breeding horses in Central America and Mexico. Some of these horses escaped and formed wild herds.

146

Eventually American Indians learned to tame and ride them, and their descendants are the tough mustangs that still live wild in some parts of the West today.

Horses were, and still are, herd animals. They are used to being dominated by a herd leader, and it is this facet of their personality that allows them to be so easily controlled by a person only a tenth their size. They are unaggressive animals whose main defense is running away. Even a well-trained horse will try to run if it is badly enough frightened. A trainer can harness the horse's great athletic abilities, developed through eons of fleeing the enemy, because their submissive nature makes obedience instinctive. Thus even a small child can guide a 1,000-pound thoroughbred over a course of jumps, or an 1,800-pound draft horse home through the fields with a wagonload of hay.

The Parrot

With their exotically colored feathers and their ability to mimic the human voice, parrots enthrall zoo visitors all over the world. Despite the fact that they are very expensive, many people keep them as pets.

Parrots are native to Asia, Africa, South America and Australia. When explorers began sailing from Europe to ports in these places they brought parrots back with them. The birds soon became status symbols for the upper classes. Amazon parrots and macaws from South America began appearing in gilded cages along with African

grey parrots, and cockatoos and parakeets from Australia.

Parrots, of course, do not really talk, at least not in the sense that humans do. They mimic sounds that they hear, presumably without understanding them. However, there have been cases of parrots that learned to say certain things at appropriate times. Konrad Lorenz, the naturalist, tells of an Amazon parrot that learned to say "good morning" in the morning and "good night" at night. Generally, parrots only learn to say things that they have heard

148

over and over again. However, they learn more quickly when they are excited. Lorenz had a free-ranging parrot that, like many birds, was afraid of large objects above it, associating them with large birds of prey. Badly frightened by the sight of a chimney sweep standing on top of one of the chimneys he liked to perch on, he thereafter would say "the chimney sweep is coming" whenever he saw the man with his top hat and brushes. He must have heard the words from Lorenz's cook, since he spoke them with her exact intonation.

Parrots make their sounds deep in their throats with their beaks closed like ventriloquists. Their beaks are not very well designed for talking, since they are really made for cracking hard foods like nuts and seeds. Their upper beaks are thick and hard; in some species they are hinged. Their lower bills are freely movable, and serve to squeeze food against the upper bill.

Confinement in a small cage is probably a great hardship to a parrot. In the wild most species live in large social groups in forests. They are strong climbers and many do not fly, but walk around on the branches of trees, using their bills as a sort of "third hand." Parrots are very long-lived—some reach 100 years, and they commonly live to an age of 50 or 60.

The Amazon parrot shows the four-clawed feet that make it and all parrots such good climbers. Two of the claws point forward, the other two backward, so they can readily grasp a branch.

The Parakeet and the Lovebird

Parakeets and lovebirds are among the smallest members of the parrot family. Both are very popular as caged birds. The kind called budgerigars are the commonest of all. They are native to Australia, where they feed on the seeds of tall grasses and congregate in flocks of hundreds of thousands around water holes. The birds live in arid areas where long periods of severe drought occur frequently. They have to take advantage of brief rainy periods to renew the species. After sufficient rain has fallen to raise a new crop of grass, the female will lay her eggs in a hole in the ground. She quickly raises 2 or 3 clutches of eggs before the drought sets in again and dries up the grass. Many parakeets die in times of drought, and even in normal times many are lost in the huge crush of birds that settles around the water holes.

Budgerigars were first exported from Australia to England by ornithologist John Gould, who exhibited them at the Crystal Palace in London's Hyde Park in 1851. They became an instant fad and were being bred all over the country within ten years. Soon breeders had created several color variations, including a blue and a yellow, in addition to the original green of the wild bird.

150

Today enough parakeets have escaped from captivity in Florida to have built up wild populations, particularly around St. Petersburg. The birds are thriving, but they are cause for some concern because of their potential as agricultural pests. The budgerigar is now North America's only wild parakeet, but there was formerly another species, the Carolina parakeet. This bird once ranged through our southern states, where it had the unfortunate habit of twisting green fruit off the trees, thus doing extensive damage to orchards. Because of this behavior it was extensively hunted, and its population dwindled until there was just one small flock remaining in Florida. Around 1920 this one, too, disappeared.

Lovebirds are about the same size as parakeets, but they are actually dwarf parrots, having longer tails than parakeets. Mates form strong bonds similar to that of the parakeet. In the wild they are natives of Africa and Madagascar. Probably because of their name they are usually kept in pairs, and therefore probably suffer less in captivity than many caged birds that are kept alone.

Many different strains of lovebird have been bred by cage-bird fanciers. Most have brightly colored heads like the pair shown here.

151

A tick (shown life size just above the title) is an inconspicuous little insect that can easily conceal itself in a plant's foliage while waiting to drop onto a mammalian host.

The Tick

Some of the early settlers in the northwestern United States came down with a mysterious disease. At first they ran a high fever and their joints hurt. Then they broke out in a rash. The disease was so bad that one-fifth of those who contracted it died. The disease was first thought to be confined to the Rocky Mountain region, hence its name: Rocky Mountain Spotted Fever. More recently it has been found in other parts of the world, but the name has stuck.

Modern medical research has shown that the disease is carried from small mammals like ground squirrels and rabbits to man, and that the carrier is the tick. In the original cases the culprit was the Rocky Mountain wood tick. Where spotted fever occurs, the disease organisms, called rickettsia, are present in the blood of the small mammals that act as carriers. The wood tick's larval stages feed on the infected blood and, as adults, the ticks then feed on the blood of larger mammals, including man. Once in

A tick engorged with blood (right, below) can weigh up to two hundred times more than an empty one. Ticks are blind, and locate their hosts by the smell of the amino acids in their sweat.

the human bloodstream the microorganisms damage the walls of blood vessels. The blood that leaks through the damaged walls causes the characteristic red spots. In severe cases, so much blood is lost that the victim dies.

Ticks generally climb up onto a bush or tree and wait for a suitable host to pass underneath. When one does, the tick drops down onto the animal and drills into its skin. It stays for about a week, filling itself with blood until it is about as big as a marble, then drops off.

Because they hold on so tightly, ticks are hard to remove. Pulling does not work. Although the blood-filled body will come off, the head remains beneath the skin, and is a possible source of infection. There are several alternatives. Campers and others who frequent forests where ticks are prevalent have devised a method that removes the whole tick: they hold the lighted end of a cigarette or an ember from the campfire close to the spot invaded by the tick. To

escape the heat, the tick backs out. It takes a steady hand and a certain amount of courage to perform the operation.

Female ticks lay their eggs at the base of plants so the young will be able to climb up and look for their own hosts. The larvae take about 3 months to hatch, and can wait as long as a year for a suitable host. Adult ticks, too, can survive for an incredibly long time without a meal of blood. Some individuals have been known to wait as long as eighteen years for a suitable host and their next meal.

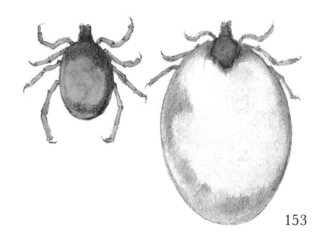

153

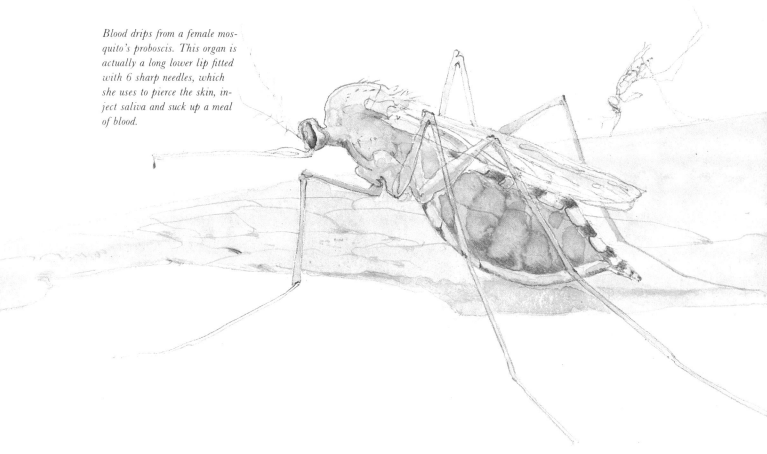

Blood drips from a female mosquito's proboscis. This organ is actually a long lower lip fitted with 6 sharp needles, which she uses to pierce the skin, inject saliva and suck up a meal of blood.

The Mosquito

Mosquitoes are close relatives of flies and are, if anything, even more annoying. The whining hum of a female mosquito hunting for a meal has kept many a would-be sleeper restless through a summer night. In addition, different species of mosquito transmit malaria, yellow fever, sleeping sickness and many other diseases. The organisms that cause these diseases live in the mosquito's salivary glands and are injected into the human bloodstream when the insects bite. Mosquitoes have probably been responsible for more human deaths than any other insect. When the French attempted to build a canal across Panama they lost more than fifty-five hundred men in nine years, largely to yellow fever, and they had to abandon the project. It is said that they lost a man for every crosstie on the Panama Railway.

Only the female mosquito feeds on blood; the male eats mostly plant juices. The female requires a blood meal before she lays her eggs. Females also tend to fly closer to the ground than males, which generally gather in swarms above trees and bushes. When a female is ready to mate she will fly up into such a swarm. The males are attracted to the exact frequency of her wingbeat; males have a sound-receiving organ on their antennae that receives vibrations only of sounds at that frequency. Experiments have shown that the male mosquitoes will respond to anything vibrating at that frequency, and will mistake even a tuning fork for a female.

Once a female has mated and filled her stomach with blood, she lays her eggs on the surface of whatever water is available: a pond, a swamp, even a puddle. The eggs float for a few days, then develop into larvae called wrigglers. After 2 or 3 weeks they pupate, then emerge as adult mosquitoes 2 or 3 days later. The adults live only a matter of weeks, during which time they mate, draw blood, lay their eggs, and begin the life cycle anew.

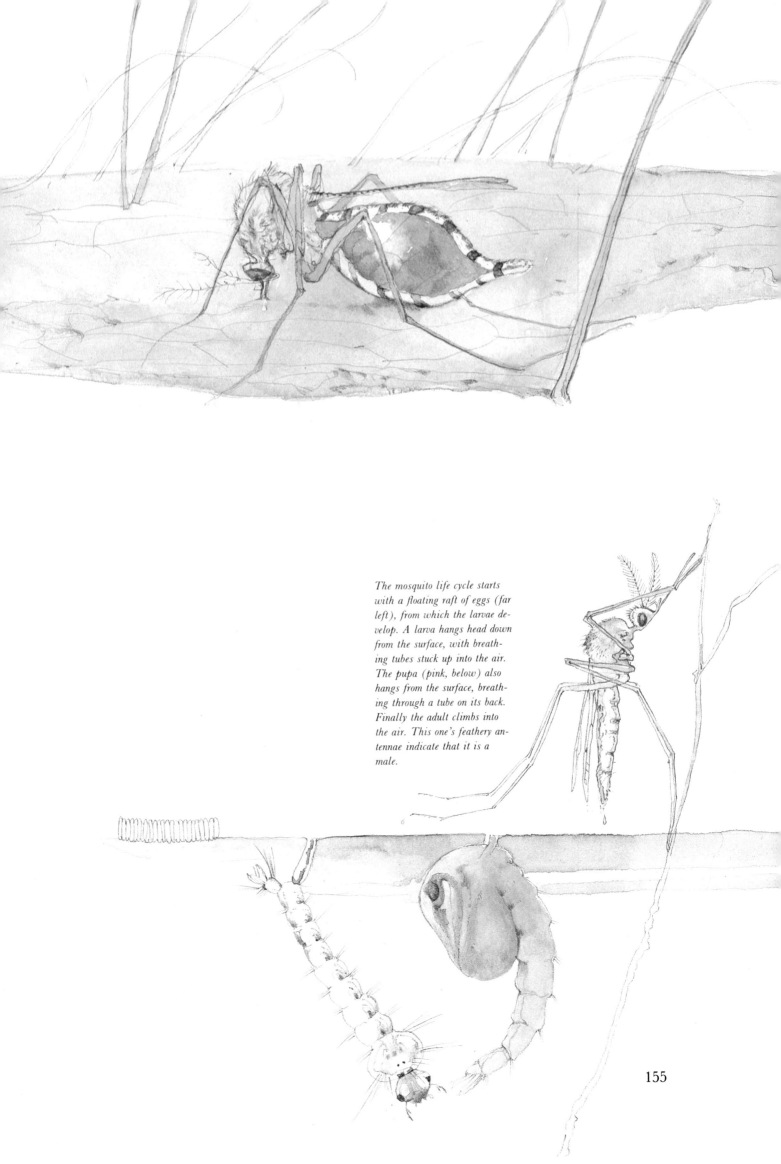

The mosquito life cycle starts with a floating raft of eggs (far left), from which the larvae develop. A larva hangs head down from the surface, with breathing tubes stuck up into the air. The pupa (pink, below) also hangs from the surface, breathing through a tube on its back. Finally the adult climbs into the air. This one's feathery antennae indicate that it is a male.

155

A huge noisy flock of starlings blackens the sky as the birds leave their sleeping place in the pink dawn.

156

The Starling

Like house sparrows, starlings were not originally native to this country, although they have become one of our most common birds. The takeover started in 1890 when sixty European starlings were released in New York City's Central Park. Another forty were set loose the next year. Evidently the environment suited them well for they began nesting and raising young. The first nest to be discovered was built, appropriately, under the eaves of the American Museum of Natural History. Starlings are well adapted to life in cities and towns, which is probably the reason they have prospered here. It took the species only sixty-nine years to spread all the way across the country, from New York City down into even the southernmost county of California.

Starlings are social birds. They come together in huge flocks, and this habit has made them somewhat of a nuisance. The birds eat mostly insects, and in this way they are beneficial to man, but they also relish soft fruits, particularly cherries. Big flocks can do serious damage to orchards. In Europe, at cherry-ripening time, people used to run through the orchards screaming, shaking rattles, ringing bells, shooting guns and exploding tins of carbide. They banged on cans and waved dead birds around. But none of this cacophony seemed to bother the starlings much. They kept

A flock of starlings feed on and argue over fallen apples in an orchard. Below, two birds demonstrate their instinctive "yawning" action, pushing the bill into the ground to open a wedge where such tidbits as worms and insects may be found.

right on eating the fruit. Today fruit growers have had better luck scaring the birds away by playing recorded distress calls from injured starlings.

The new fall feathers starlings grow are white-tipped, so during autumn and early winter starlings appear to be spotted. But the white gradually wears off, and by spring the birds have nearly reached their normal summer color of glossy black with iridescent patches shining green and purple. Most starlings winter-over where they breed, but some do migrate. The feathers of these migrating birds are especially worn.

Starlings, like their close relatives the mynahs, are excellent imitators and can be

A city starling sits on a window casing singing a song that consists largely of imitations of other bird's songs, as well as a few city noises.

taught to talk. They mimic the songs of other birds, as well as such sounds as the buzzing of a saw or the squeaking of a rusty gate hinge. They also call to each other constantly while they are flying or roosting at night. The noise of a large flock roosting on the trees outside a house can be extremely annoying, and the mess of the droppings from several hundred birds can irritate even the most patient homeowner.

Starlings are strong flyers, and their large flocks have developed an effective method of dealing with attacks by hawks. Ordinarily the flock flies in a big, loose formation, but at the sight of a large bird flying overhead the flock tightens into a dense pack.

The hawk is then afraid to dive down for a kill because it would be injured or knocked out of the sky by the closely packed starlings. For a long time no one understood how a big flock of starlings could coordinate its movements so perfectly. When they fly, the birds all seem to change direction simultaneously. But slow-motion movies have shown that one bird turns first, with the others following as a group. Because the flock follows the leader so quickly it is thought that the birds turn by reflex in response to the first bird, rather than by making a conscious decision to follow.

159

The Sparrow

Many of our most common birds and animals are not truly native to our shores, but have been introduced by man for a variety of reasons. Because these introduced species do not have a niche in the local ecology, they often fail; they cannot fit into the balance of species already present. But for the same reason they may do abnormally well, pushing out native species as they multiply. In such cases it is usually not a question of an open ecological niche, but rather the absence of a suitable predator to keep the newly introduced animal in check.

One introduction that has been extremely successful is the house, or English, sparrow. Eight of these birds were first brought to this country by Nicholas Pike, director of New York's Brooklyn Institute, who then released them in the Institute's botanical garden. The eight did not do well, but two years later another group was released in a cemetery in Brooklyn, and these thrived and multiplied.

House sparrows are a particularly social species, feeding and flying together in big groups. When males are courting females they tumble around in the dust holding their heads and their tails up. As many as ten males may chase and circle one female.

160

English sparrows have adapted themselves to a lifestyle that fits closely with man's. Probably they have associated closely with man since he first turned from hunter to farmer. From the Middle East, where agriculture began, the sparrows followed man and his cultivated crops across Europe and into England, whence they came to us.

English sparrows prefer to build their nests in birdhouses, but they also nest inside buildings, under eaves, behind shutters and, if necessary, in a hole in a tree. They build nests out of grasses and straw, and eat seeds and insects. Once a great source of food for them was the undigested oats that passed through horses and ended up in their manure. When horses were an important source of transportation in cities, English sparrows were even more common there than they are now.

Another introduced sparrow is the Eurasian tree sparrow, but its American history has taken a very different course from that of the English sparrow. In 1870, twelve tree sparrows were released in LaFayette Park in St. Louis. These birds did well and began raising offspring. They spread steadily for five years until English sparrows were introduced into the same area. The new arrivals were more aggressive and stronger, and they began to take over the tree sparrows' territory. As a result the tree sparrows' spread was halted, and the species is today confined to a small area in Missouri and Illinois. It otherwise might have spread dramatically.

The European tree sparrow can be distinguished from the English sparrow by its rust-colored head.

161

The Chipmunk

With a flash of stripes, a red-gold chipmunk scuttles over the autumn leaves, storing food for winter. Chipmunks are among our most familiar animals because they are active mostly during the day, when we can easily observe them. Also, they become quite tame once they become accustomed to humans. In many campgrounds they will unhesitatingly approach people, hoping for a handout.

Chipmunks spend a great deal of their time stocking their winter larders. One observer watched a group transporting food

Three chipmunks gather acorns under an oak tree (left), while another, his cheek pouches filled with food for storage, ducks into his burrow (right).

into storage. During three days they accumulated sixty-five pounds of nuts and corn. The transportation of food is made more efficient through the use of their 2 large cheek pouches. When these pockets are filled to capacity, they are almost as large as the animal's whole head. Being able to carry so much food at one time gives chipmunks a selective advantage. It cuts down on the number of trips that they must make from a food source to their burrow. These trips are extremely dangerous, because they expose the animals to a wide range of predators, from hawks to house cats.

Eastern chipmunks begin mating in March, and the mating season extends throughout the summer. Gestation takes 31 days, at the end of which time the female produces a litter of between 2 and 8 babies. Despite their small size, chipmunks live about 5 years. Western chipmunks have only one breeding period a year, producing their babies in April and May. They are striped like the eastern variety, but tend to be yellow rather than red.

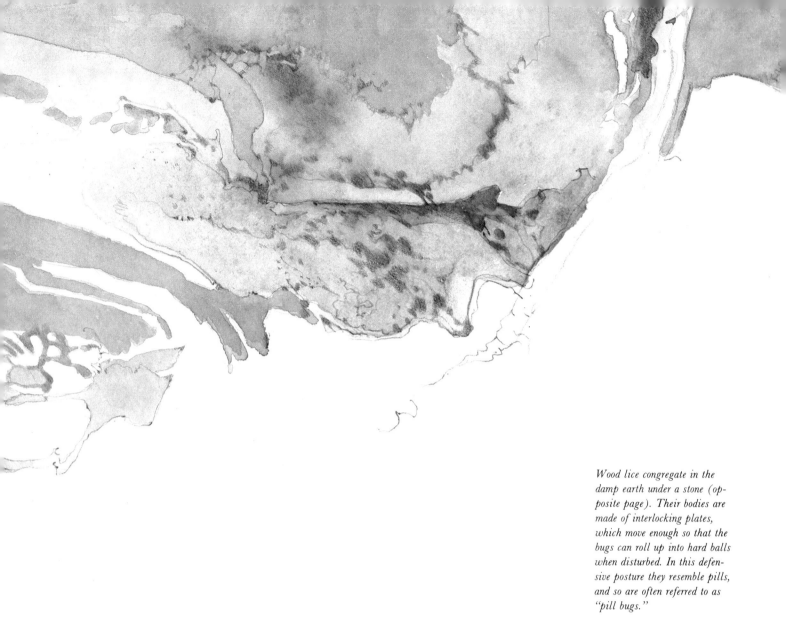

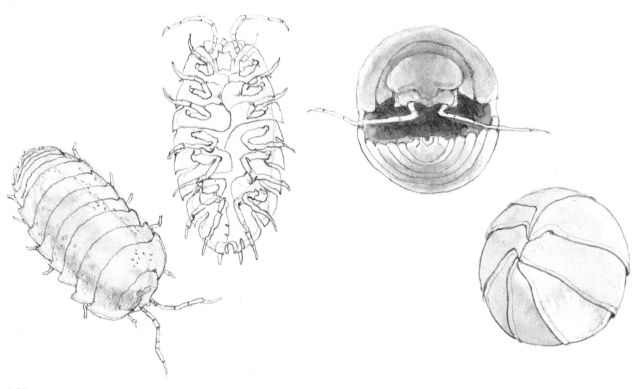

Wood lice congregate in the damp earth under a stone (opposite page). Their bodies are made of interlocking plates, which move enough so that the bugs can roll up into hard balls when disturbed. In this defensive posture they resemble pills, and so are often referred to as "pill bugs."

164

The Wood Louse

People who like to take walks in the woods, and gardeners who poke around and disturb rocks in damp corners, are the most likely observers of wood lice. These creatures are not insects but crustaceans—relatives of shrimp and lobsters. Like their marine cousins, wood lice have bodies made of interlocking segments, each with a hard covering and a set of legs. The wood louse is one of only a handful of crustacean species that have moved ashore—most still live in water—but it has not become so terrestrial that it can forsake water entirely. It still needs a damp environment because it uses gills on its legs to breathe. It can conserve moisture by rolling itself into a ball; the hard plates on its back cut down the evaporation of water. The ability to roll itself into a "pill" discourages ants and milli-

pedes, its major predators. As a further defense, the wood louse can exude a foul-smelling substance.

Although wood lice are often found in large groups, they do not congregate for social reasons. Rather, they are drawn individually to the same dark, humid spots that support the foods they need. They feed mostly at night on plants, fruit, rotting vegetation and even carrion.

Female wood lice have a pouch on the underside of their abdomens called a marsupium, where they carry their eggs and their newly hatched young for a few days. As they grow, wood lice must shed their outer covering several times. This leaves them defenseless until their new covering hardens. At this stage, many are lost to the cannibalism of their own brothers and sisters.

The Canary

A male canary standing up on his perch and singing his heart out has brought tears of pleasure to many a lonely old person. Canaries are pretty to look at and to listen to, and easy to feed. In many ways they are the perfect cage bird.

Canaries are named for their original home, the Canary Islands, which lie off the northwest coast of Africa. They were discovered there by Spanish conquerers toward the end of the fifteenth century. The soldiers brought them back to Europe where they quickly became so popular that the supply could not keep up with the demand. However, fanciers soon found that the birds were perfectly willing to breed and raise their young in captivity.

As the birds spread throughout Europe, breeders in different countries began modifying the original strain in various ways. The French bred birds with curly feathers, the Germans specialized in song, the Belgians modified the shape, the Dutch concentrated on color. Luckily for all the breeders, the wild stock they started with seemed to have a diverse collection of genes, which allowed them to select for all these different characteristics. In addition, breeders have intensified some traits by crossing canaries with finches. In this way many new colors have been brought into the breed.

Wild birds do not sing as beautifully as those specifically bred for song, but they

Tame canaries retain their wild instinct to nurture their young, which makes them easy birds to raise in captivity.

certainly have the genetic capability, as indicated by an experiment performed by the animal behaviorist Nikolaas Tinbergen. Tinbergen allowed a captive canary to raise a bullfinch baby. When the bullfinch grew up, it sang a perfect canary song, which it had learned by imitating other canaries raised in the same room. The adult bullfinch was then mated with another bullfinch, and their offspring also sang the canary song, learned this time from the father bullfinch. Even the original bullfinch's grandchildren sang like canaries, having learned in turn from their fathers. No wild bullfinch ever sang a canary's song, but the capability was there, and Tinbergen showed that the song was not a part of the bird's genetic makeup, but rather learned by each succeeding generation.

Two English strains of canary, the Yorkshire (yellow) and the Border Fancy (right), show how far breeders have removed cultivated birds from the original wild bird (above).

167

*Cottontail babies cluster around
the entrance to their burrow.
Since rabbits have little means
of defense, they are wary and
must seek safety underground.*

Rabbits can run at speeds of up to twenty-five miles per hour to escape predators.

The Rabbit

Rabbits and their relatives, pikas and hares, belong to the Lagomorpha, an order that has been something of a puzzle to classifying biologists. Although rabbits look a great deal like rodents, such as rats, mice and squirrels, and were once thought to belong to their order, there are some striking differences. One of the most compelling is found in their blood types. There is no similarity between those of rabbits and rodents, but rabbit blood does bear certain similarities to that of hoofed animals, such as deer and cows. Another piece of evidence for a distant relationship between these seemingly disparate groups comes from rabbits' odd habit of eating some of their droppings. Rabbits excrete two kinds of pellets, one of which is covered with mucus and is nutritious, and the other of which is dry. They eat the moist droppings and pass them through their digestive system a second time to extract more of the nutrients. This process may well be analogous to a ruminant's cud chewing, which also allows the food additional opportunity for digestion.

Rabbits have long been a favorite animal of sportsmen, who enjoy hunting them. Unfortunately, colonial English sportsmen have been responsible for the devastation of some parts of Australia and New Zealand because they introduced rabbits as game. The rabbits thrived, multiplying faster than the hunters could shoot them, and ate so much that they severely damaged the sheep industry. In addition, sailors dropped off rabbits on many islands so they would have a ready source of fresh meat when they landed there again. In places where there were few or no natural predators, the rabbits consequently multiplied and stripped away all the vegetation.

Even in Roman times, some islands in

169

the Mediterranean where rabbits were released to grow meat for the upper classes became so overrun that the inhabitants had to beg the emperor to provide them with less infested lands.

Rabbits multiply fast because they have a rapid reproductive rate. Common cottontail rabbits in northern regions have 3 to 5 litters a season, averaging 4 babies per litter. In a few weeks the babies are themselves mature enough to breed. Where conditions are favorable for many of the young to survive—in places with plenty of feed and few predators—large populations can build up fast. Farmers who raise domestic rabbits for food have found that one pair of rabbits and their offspring will produce more meat in a year than a beef steer.

Under domestication rabbits have taken on a great variety of shapes and sizes. Many breeds have been created to provide meat that is light and flavorful, quite similar to chicken. Angora rabbits have long, silky hair, which makes soft wool yarns. A great many breeds have been created by fanciers interested in rabbits' colors and shapes, which they display at county fairs.

Mother rabbits sometimes carry their babies as cats do, by the scruff of the neck.

170

Rabbit droppings covered with mucus contain valuable nutrients. Rabbits eat and redigest them.

Domestic rabbits range in size from the Flemish giant, which weighs more than 13 pounds, to the tiny 1½-pound Polish rabbit.

171

A great horned owl stares with regal dignity. One of America's largest owls, it can have a wingspread of up to 6 feet and consume animals as big as a full-grown rabbit.

The Owl

The soft cry of an owl hooting at night is one of the scariest sounds nature has to offer. It seems to come from nowhere, a disembodied voice, coming first from one direction, then from another, boding ill.

Of course there is nothing supernatural about an owl. It is merely a bird that is magnificently adapted to its lifestyle of hunting at night. Both the owl's vision and its hearing are acute. Owl eyes are quite large in proportion to the size of the bird—a snowy owl is about 2 feet tall, but its eyes are as large as a man's. Owl retinas are rich in rods, the light-receiving cells responsible for seeing in dim light. However, many owls also have numerous cones. These visual cells allow color vision, and also serve to form sharp images in bright light. Owls have a well-developed third eyelid, which they can close to protect their eyes from light that is too bright. Like those of most birds, owls' eyes are fixed, and they have to move their head to change their field of vision. Many

A young great horned owl pauses for a moment before eating a rat that it has killed.

people think that owls can turn their heads in a full circle. Of course if they could their heads would twist right off. But owls *can* turn their heads 270 degrees—three-quarters of the way around—then spin their heads back too fast for the human eye to follow.

An owl's hearing is perhaps even more acute than its vision, and plays a big part in locating prey in the dark. Its ears are set inside feathered openings in the sides of its head, which can be opened into funnel shapes that focus incoming sound waves. Many owls have one ear different in shape and size from the other, so that they receive

173

Long-eared owls are one of a whole group of "horned" owls. The horns are not actually ears, but tufts of feathers. Their function may be to help the owls recognize one another as members of the same species.

174

sound waves slightly differently. This difference allows the owl to determine what direction the sound is coming from. Even the disc-shaped face of the owl serves to focus waves of sound, in the manner of a parabolic radar receiver.

One of the attributes that make owls such efficient predators is the ability to fly silently and catch their prey by surprise. The noise that air makes passing over the wings of most birds is muted in owls by the sawtoothed edge of their leading wing feathers, which breaks up the noisy currents of air.

There are two main families of owl: barn owls, and what are known as typical owls. The typical owls inhabit almost every part of the world except Antarctica. Barn owls are also widespread, although in this country they are most common in the southern states. They differ from typical owls in the shape of their face—heart-shaped rather than oval—and have square rather than rounded tails.

Screech owls do not really screech but have a soft, mournful call that rises and then slips down the scale.

175

Index

milk production *(cont.)*
  of goats, 122
millipedes, 92–93
  as predator of wood louse, 165
mites
  as prey of daddy-longlegs, 64
  and spiders, 28
moles, *34,* 35–37
molluscs, 82–84
monarch butterfly, 14–15, *16, 17*
monogamy
  of deer mice, *48*
  of swans, *116,* 117
Mormon locust plague, 140
mosquitoes, 88, 154, *155*
  predators of, 110, 124
moths, 15–17
  as prey of purple martin, 124
moulting
  of dragonflies and damselflies,
    53
  of ducks, 19
  of spiders, 31
Muscovy duck, 20
mustangs, 147
mynahs, 158

N

Napoleon, army of
  homing pigeons used by, 41
  louse-spread typhus in, 101
National Audubon Society, 135
navigation sense
  of bats, 95
  of moles, 36
  of pigeons, 41
Norwegian duns, *146*

O

ocelot, 114
orchards
  parakeet damage to, 151
  starling damage to, 157–158
Orthoptera, 140
owls, 172–175

P

Panama Canal yellow fever epi-
    demic, 154
parakeets, 148, 150

parrots, 148–149
parthogenesis, lizard reproduc-
    tion by, 133
peacock, *see* peafowl
peafowl, 38–39
peck order of chickens, 103
Pekin duck, 19, *20, 21*
pets
  bats as, 97
  crows as, 73
  goats as, 122–123
  guinea pigs as, 86, 87
  raccoons as, 79
  squirrels as, 12
  see also cats; dogs; domestica-
    tion of animals
pheasants, 38, 103
Pied Piper of Hamelin, 139
pigeons, 40–41
pikas, 169
Pike, Nicholas, 160
plants
  damage to, by animals, *see*
    damage by animals
  fertilization by bees, 8
platys, 110–111
Pliny the Elder on snails, 82
pointer, 67
poisonous secretion of centipedes,
    93
population explosions
  of locusts, 140
  of meadow mice, 49
  of rabbits, 169–170
prehistoric representations
  of horses in cave paintings, 145
  of pigeons in Iran, 41
protective legislation for snowy
    egrets, 135
prussic acid secretion of centi-
    pedes, 93
Przewalski's horse, 145

Q

queens in insect societies, 9, 43–
    44, 107, 109
quills, goose, 119

R

rabbits, 168–171, *172*
  predators of, 61, *172*

Rocky Mountain Spotted
    Fever carried by, 152
rabies, 95
raccoons, 78–79
radar-like sound reception of
    owls, 175
rats, 136–139
  flea infestation of, 55
  as pests, 120, 136
  predators of, 76, 173
  role in human disease, 55, 136,
    138
ravens, 72, 73
red jungle fowl, 103
regenerative capacity of earth-
    worms, 63
repellent secretions
  of daddy-longlegs, 65
  of toads, 3
reproduction rate of flies, 89
retrievers, 67
rickettsia, 152
robin, 6–7, 124
rock doves, 40
Rocky Mountain Spotted Fever,
    152–153
Roman civilization
  pet squirrels in, *12*
  use of pigeons by, 41

S

St. Bernard, 66, 68
salamanders, 22
saliva, toad's defensive use of, 3
samoyed, 67
scavenger role of chickens, 104
schistosomiasis, snail spread of,
    83–84
scorpions, 28
sexton beetles, *130,* 131
sheep ticks as prey of magpies, 77
shepherds, 67
Shetland pony, *146*
ships, rats on, 136
shrews, 35
Siamese cat, 114
silk spinning of spiders, 28–29
skin shedding of toads, 4
skunks, *36*
slavery in ant societies, 45
sleeping sickness, mosquito-
    borne, 154